Harold Hoefle

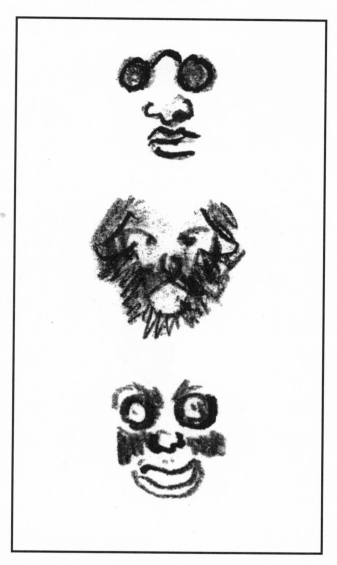

# The Mountain Clinic

We acknowledge the support of the Canada Council for the Arts, the Ontario Arts Council, the Government of Ontario through the Ontario Media Development Corporation and the Government of Canada through the Book Publishing Industry Development Program for our publishing activities.

Parts of this book first appeared in *Exile*, *Front&Centre*, *Grain* and the anthology *Telling Stories*. "Flaco Was Here" originally appeared in the chapbook *Spray Job*. An early version of "The Mountain Clinic" was a finalist in the *Malahat Review* 2008 Novella Contest; an early version of this book won an Honourable Mention for the 2003 David Adams Richards Award sponsored by the Writers' Federation of New Brunswick. The author would like to thank Matthew Firth of Black Bile Press, Mark Anthony Jarman and the friends who helped to shape various drafts.

ISBN 978 0 7780 1325 9 (hardcover)
ISBN 978 0 7780 1327 3 (softcover)

Cover art by James Ensor
Edited by Mark Anthony Jarman
Book design by Michael Macklem

Printed in Canada

PUBLISHED IN CANADA BY OBERON PRESS

Canada Council
for the Arts
Conseil des Arts
du Canada

ONTARIO ARTS COUNCIL
CONSEIL DES ARTS DE L'ONTARIO

# Contents

For Amy

# 1. Trail

In my father's shop, I swept sawdust. That was my Saturday job in 1966, when I was seven. I remember some things from that spring workday, and imagine others.

"Here," he said, and tipped the broom handle. It was bigger than me and I fumbled it, then caught hold.

"Remember," he added, tapping the concrete floor with his shoe, "to push out from here and sweep to the wall. Get *all* the sawdust. Get under the machines. And don't forget the rat."

My father brought his cologne-scented cheek down to mine, and his checked shirt also smelled good. His hair was smooth and black, his grey-green eyes like lake water.

"The rat's new," he said, his whisper tickling my ear. "Don't play with him. He's white, the kind with no teeth. He just wiggles on his back and rubs his sides against the machines. If he knows you like him, he'll chase you all day."

My father's shoulders rose and dropped.

"I close my door so he can't come in. He's bad luck—he makes people lazy."

My father turned around and disappeared in his office.

I held the broom and stared at a tall can stuffed with wooden slats. The rat might've been crouched in its shadow. I was afraid. The shop was quiet, listening. I heard my father's voice in his office; he must've been on the phone. Broom in hand, I looked around, at the high ceiling, painted-beige brick walls, propeller fan blades, tubular lights and round white ducts that rose from the machines to the ceiling like tilted metal trees. The shop seemed like a huge birch forest. At least, so I remember it. In reality, it was a 3000-square-foot concrete box, about the size of a small backyard. The building housed F.S. Windows, Ltd.—my father's proud achievement. In that spring of 1966, Franz Schwende had already owned the company for over a year. Of course, he wanted success. That's why he left Austria after the war; that's why my mother left the same country. They met at Toronto's Edelweiss Club, an Austrian meeting-place where all those dreamers gathered to eat goulash and schnitzel, to drink heavy and dance light.

That workday, I did the usual: put my head down and swept. I had my own style, a combination of the way I played road hockey and imagined driving. I gripped the handle, my hands a foot apart, and steered the broom everywhere. Actually I raced, speeding after every speck of orange sawdust that coated the floor and formed trails around tables and machines. My sprint only paused when I found things like brackets, nails or tape measures. I returned them all to the tables, so the workers wouldn't get into trouble. Ken and Derek were good to me. Once they came to our house and Ken made me laugh by holding a pencil in his sucked-in cheek. Later, Derek showed me how to stand on my head by using a wall. He'd hold my ankles and coach me. When blood rushed to my face, I knew how to stay calm and balance myself.

My sweep was halfway done when my left hand started to sting. I looked—raw red circles mottled my fingers. The blisters hurt and it was hard to grip the broom, yet I still wanted to do another sweep, to make the floor gleam like it did on my first workday, the first Saturday my mother let me help my father: the day I met his challenge.

On that face-freezing January morning, we walked into the shop and my father said the sweeping was finished *only* when you could lick the floor and taste pure concrete, clean enough that you could swallow your spit and not retch. At our shutdown time of five o'clock, and right in front of him, I dropped to my knees, put my mouth to the floor and licked. I probably did it for just two seconds before he yanked me up by my armpits. His voice quavering, he told me to *Never, never do that again.* Then he looked away and spoke again, though in a much softer tone, one that sounded hollow, like

8

it had lost a shouting match. "My idea was stupid. I'm sorry."

That happened three months ago. Now my hand stung, but I still swept a few sawdust piles into the dustpan and tipped the orange load into the garbage. There were bandages in his office: I could get some and attack the flecks again, finish my job. The problem, though, was my father. He was in the office, and what if my knock angered him?

I walked around the shop.

I counted the saw blades on wall nails, felt the sandpaper rolls, and stared at graffiti Ken and Derek had scrawled on their machines. The square wall clock said 2.30. Scattered on the floor were my little pyramids of sawdust. I shuffled toward the office door, but I approached from the side just like I did on a breakaway: I'd always angle in on the goalie, because heading straight at the net would make me feel small and exposed.

I periscoped my head up to the office window. My father didn't see me. Sweat shone on his face under the ceiling bulb and he was walking back and forth, the phone cord trailing him like a leash. He shouted. The gush of anger staggered me back a step, as if I'd been pushed.

"Damn what he says! *Arschloch!*"

Minutes later, I was slowly pushing the broom along a wall when he approached me, his shirt pulled out over his belt and his glasses tilted to one side.

"Walter, I have to go out—keep working, okay?"

"Get me hockey cards, Daddy? And an ice cream bar?"

He didn't move, and I tried to see his eyes behind his glasses. He leaned over me, his right hand coming up like it was going to muss my hair or touch my shoulder. Instead he strode off, got his coat off the hook and rushed outside. I heard our car start, then its engine, then nothing. I entered his office.

I'd been in there before and had checked everything out: the wide window with its brown curtains sewn by my mother; the full-length mirror; the corkboard papered with work-site drawings; the black filing cabinet; the shelf of supplier and phone books; and the desk with papers stacked neatly at its back edge, a thick blue German-English dictionary in a corner. But today the desk was a mess of torn pages and crumpled carbons. A printed page was moist with coffee from an overturned cup. Papers lay on the floor. I wanted to pick everything up, but I couldn't do that. I pulled on a desk drawer instead. Locked. I tried another. Locked. Another. Locked. The last one slid toward me.

I took out a Montreal Expo '67 baseball cap—but it wasn't 1967 yet. I was confused. Okay, I knew my father travelled to Montreal and spoke with people at an aluminum factory, because he wanted to start aluminum window production. But he, my mother and I were faithful supporters of our home hockey team, the Maple Leafs—*les Canadiens* were our enemies. I brought the cap to my nose and smelled it, caught a whiff of something alien.

I bent down to see what else was in the drawer. Big surprise: papers. I pulled one out, and was staring at words I didn't know when a car pulled up to the shop. I shoved the cap and papers back in the drawer, shut it and sped to my broom. In he walked.

A passing truck shook the concrete floor.

"Sun's out," he said, strolling toward me. He pointed at an iron ladder bolted to the back wall. "Time to see the roof."

I stared at the ladder's height, my body like a bottle filling with fear. I felt hands gripping my shoulders. I was turned around and marched to the wall.

"Climb slow," my father cautioned, "then unhook the hatch. The bolt isn't heavy. And you don't need your coat."

After a gentle shove I was doing it, grabbing the rungs and telling myself not to be afraid, not to look down and not to think I couldn't open the door to a different world. I climbed, wondering if the rat was watching us. Whether it cared.

I reached the deadbolt and its plate smeared with grease.

The bolt moved easily. I stuck my head into air and blinked. Spread before me was an expanse of flat and peaked roofs, some surfaces broken by vents spewing smoke or steam. I hoisted myself onto the roof, the wet snow stinging my blisters and reminding me I hadn't asked for bandages. Still, I couldn't stop staring north and west: beyond the last buildings were hills and fields patched with snow, stretches of grey earth and trees, black roads and driveways, white farmhouses, and dark green pines the colour of my Uncle Karl's loden jacket. I blinked again in the brightness, as if my eyes were trying to drink up the sun and there was too much. Parked cars and windows flashed it back at me. On a silver pole, a red-and-white Canadian flag fluttered, collapsed, fluttered again, and I could hear the drone of traffic. Then I saw my father's severed head above the hatch. I wanted to run up and put him back together, but that was impossible.

"Look," he said, once he stood on the roof and my arms pincered his waist. He pointed north. "It goes on and on, just farms and land."

He smoked while we looked in the same direction, and for the first time I was drawn to the purplish blue of far hills.

My father flicked his cigarette over the roof and led me to its middle. In seconds I was airborne.

Fingers clamped on my wrists, he twirled me in circles, dizzying me. I could either look down at the rushing roof or force my head up and stare at his thighs. I wondered how he could do this without dizzying himself, yet he didn't stop. Instead of becoming more afraid, I started to trust the fingers roped around my wrists. I was weightless. I could fly! For what seemed like an hour but was likely a minute or so, I *did* fly, until I felt my father wobble, my flight slow down. I almost scraped my knees on the roof, but I touched down feet first. He swayed for a second, righted himself and thrust a hand into his pocket. Held out a fist.

I pried open his fingers and found a silver coin with a caribou head: my weekly wage, enough for caramels and popsicles.

"Daddy, are you rich?"

He didn't hear me, or he acted that way. Head back, he was watching a long V of geese, their flight a black scribble moving across the sky. He said something.

"What?" I asked.

"*Alles war besser zu Hause.*"

"I don't understand."

He mumbled again, and I thought he said "things were better back home." My father reached again for his cigarettes. Behind him the sky was losing its blueness, as if some god had poured pails of dirty water into it, diluting it into a weak grey soup.

"I'm not rich yet," he said, toeing some snow. "In my hand is a house, a car, a shop, and machines. But the bank and government kick me around like a soccer ball." He puffed on his cigarette, looked at the sky and shrugged. "You know what your Opa says? The man who's lived through two wars?"

A crow blasted by me at eye-level, and I thought of cartoon bullets on TV.

"Let's go," said my father, and led me back to the hatch.

"What does Opa say?"

"What?"

"Opa—what does he say?"

"One day, everything will happen."

I didn't understand, and I wanted to ask about the hockey cards and ice cream bar, even though it seemed too late.

In five minutes the shop was locked and he was reversing our car into the road, his left hand on the wheel and his right behind my head. Soon we were driving past snow pocked by gravel, past slush trenched by other wheels.

"Daddy, did you get hockey cards?"

He said nothing. We headed south and got on the 401, the wide highway that skimmed the northern edge of Toronto. At our Warden exit he didn't turn, we just hurtled westward.

"Check your coat," he said, passing cars on his right.

I groped in my pockets.

"The inside one, *Dummkopf!*"

I unzipped my inner pocket and felt something flat. A white envelope. I ripped off the flap and took out two tickets: Toronto Maple Leafs vs. Montreal Canadiens. Maple Leaf Gardens. 8 PM.

I'd never been to a game, but that night I went and saw far-away figures glide up and down the white ice. I was much more interested in the ice cream bars my father bought us— the game bored me. I never went to another one with him, and I only went to the shop once more, when my father's father came to see us in July. I still don't understand why my mother refused to let me work another day until Opa's arrival from Austria. She wouldn't answer when I stood in the kitchen and begged to know. I asked my father too, but he just grunted something about "the boss" and went into the yard with a beer and his cigarettes. So. Months passed. Opa came for a few sweat-drip weeks. Soon after his visit, one morning my father left for work and never came back.

I live in Montreal, and in a few months I'll leave for Opa's village to help celebrate his hundredth birthday: 21 August, 1996. Another August event, this one in Austria, 30 years after my father's disappearance. You don't choose the red-letter days on your mental calendar. Today, and for most days before I go to Opa's village, I'll sit here at my window desk and examine the father relics: a silver-plated tiepin; a dark-faced watch; a US Army mess-kit knife; and photographs, their moods and poses. Along with these objects are a *Toronto Star* article and my own scrawled notes. Last December I requested the police occurrence report on my father's disappearance, and a woman officer with the Freedom of Information Unit continues to assure me it'll arrive soon. Now I pick up each desk object, turn it over, bring it to my eyes. If there are words, I try to puzzle out the unspokens, the whispers.

Many mysteries still surround the disappearance. Yes, the newspaper article gives some clues: a business acquaintance sighted my father in Toronto months after he left; he owed money to the government; he wasn't getting enough orders to pay his bills; a car registered in his name was found wrecked near Kingston. The article also offers melodrama: a front-page photo of my mother weeping into a handkerchief. The caption reads: "She's sure he's alive—somewhere."

I don't recall her confidence, but I can still hear my father's favourite commands, his ways of making me join his escapes. Perhaps to legitimize them in my mother's eyes.

"Walter, get in the car. Bring your jacket."

"Walter, we're going for a walk. Get your running shoes."

"Walter, where's your bathing suit?"

He'd say something like that and we'd be gone, speeding down a road.

Once we went to a park. People were playing tennis, and the slow *pock-pock* followed us to the swings and the yellow slide. I chose speed and he chose rhythm, and we sometimes shouted to each other across the playground. I loved my whooshing plummet and how, when my feet hit the sand, puffs of dust sprayed into the air. After a while my father came to get me. He waited at the bottom, and when I landed he took my hand and we began the walk through the grass, back to the car. The sky had purple in it.

"Why do you like the slide?" he said.

"It's faster than the swings, and the sides stop you from falling off."

"But you always start over," he said, and pulled my hand so we'd walk faster.

My father and I walked, played, swam. Anything to get away from the house. We sometimes drove to the lake, down the long Scarborough avenues, and often we'd stop for ice cream, especially on night drives, when every road wore a necklace of lit street lamps. My father waved his cigarette while he talked, ashes falling like grey confetti into his lap.

14

Another outing of ours was the jaunt north to the Stouffville airport. We'd park and leave the car, hook our fingers into the perimeter fence, press our noses into its mesh. The fence was so long you couldn't see its ends. My father and I would stand still and watch the Cessnas lift off, buzz into the sky and vanish.

One August morning in 1966, when my mother told me again to eat, I stopped the spoon at my mouth. She didn't notice. She was looking out the window at the pears and plums that bent our backyard trees. Near my head, the radio droned the morning traffic. I reached up to turn down the dial, the phone rang in the hall and my mother ran. But she never ran: she was a lady, her neck always swathed in a scarf, her eyes shadowed in blue, her mouth coloured a shiny red.

"*Wo ist er?*" she said.

She whispered something and hung up.

"Where's Daddy?" I asked.

"Last night he worked late. He slept at the shop."

My mother looked at me, her face flushed, her lips a minus sign. And her face changed: all the skin and muscles relaxed into a smile. I could see her teeth, perfectly white and straight.

"Just finish eating, Walter. Then you can go outside."

She started to wipe down the kitchen counter with the dishrag, her arm making vigorous arcs. I watched her back, not trusting her sudden niceness. Still, I ate my food and went down to the side-door landing for my hockey stick. Other sticks scraped the road. A shot hit a post, made a hollow *tink*.

Outside, Kevin checked Marty over a curb, knocking him onto a lawn. After a few words I joined Kevin's team. He played rough and was a notorious ball-hog, yet that day he surprised me with a pass on a two-on-one. I missed the net, but he kept on setting me up. I managed to pick a few corners, and once jammed a shot between the goalie's pads. Soon after that a car turned into our crescent and made a wide turn into my driveway. A grey-haired man in a suit rapped on our door, which swung open. My mother was still dressed in her apron. The man went past her into our house, and the door was shut.

"Who's that?" Marty wondered.

Chin resting on my stick, I stared at the blue car in our driveway and thought about how my father always came home after work.

"My dad's friend," I lied.

Late-morning heat pounded into us, but we played for another hour. Sweat soaked my T-shirt. My legs stiffened into stone. No-one stickhandled anymore, we just flicked the ball to each other and took long slapshots the goalies brushed aside like flies.

The man left my house and my mother followed. He got into the car and his hand came through the window, but she wouldn't take it. Instead she gripped his door and shouted something I couldn't make out. She jabbed her finger at him. Finally the man backed his car out of our driveway. Sunglasses hid his eyes, but I could tell he was looking at everyone's face because he drove slowly, swivelling his head until he passed us.

Later I sat in our kitchen and gulped down a glass of juice. My mother hovered, her scarf trailing in the air as she went from counter to fridge, fridge to window. Her eyes were red. The police had found Daddy's car.

"Where?" I cried, and looked at the wall behind her, the plaques of smiling blondes and their Austrian proverbs. *Cleanliness is Godliness. The Guest is King. Home is Heaven.*

"On a street near the lake," she said in a flat, controlled tone, then she scraped cooked carrots into a pan and clattered it on the stove. "Near the racetrack. His clothes were folded up in the back seat." She twisted the dial to high.

I must've thought about what she was telling me. She didn't explain it. My mother usually answered questions with a shut mouth, turned back, shouted command, or the threat of playtime denied.

Her arm grazed mine when she settled utensils and a plate of mashed potatoes, ham, and carrots in front of me, her scent mixing with the food smells.

"He was a great swimmer," I said. "Up at Lake Simcoe—"

I started to eat. I was starving.

"He hardly went in—you know that." Her face bunched up and she closed her eyes. "But maybe this time. Maybe he knocked his head on a rock." She started to make squeaking noises, her shoulders moving up and down.

"Who knows," she said, her voice breaking.

"Mommy!" I stood up, hitting my hand on the table's edge. I ran and pushed my face into her stomach.

She stopped crying, wiped some crumbs from my lips and ate them.

On the following afternoons, at about 5.30, I still set the table for three. I lifted the white plates down from the cupboard and slid them into their spots. I put out the napkins, forks, knives and spoons. The clean glasses beside the plates. After a few days, my mother told me not to lay a place for my father, but I did anyway. Then the plates felt heavy, and I was always tired after road hockey. Soon I set the table for two.

Not long after my father disappeared, the police returned our Volkswagen and my mother drove me to the plaza. She held my hand as we went to stores to find me some new pants. She begged clerks and managers for discounts: "I'm a widow with this small boy, my husband had no life insurance." After we left one store, I asked her what widow meant, but she just squeezed my hand harder and pulled me into another store with glaring lights. Later that afternoon she went shopping again, this time alone.

I remember waiting: I knelt on the couch, held aside our front curtains and watched the crescent. All the arriving cars turned into other driveways: other fathers were coming home from work, other mothers from shopping. The crescent

17

stilled. Supper-time passed. No-one came out to play in the last light. The sky went pink and the phone didn't ring and I wondered whether my mother had had an accident. Arms wrapped around my chest, I pressed my face against the window. No cars or people appeared in the street and only the sky changed, into a mud colour. A porch light came on. Then another. And another.

After dark, headlights swung into our driveway.

She was lifting grocery bags out of the trunk when I wiped my face and ran toward her.

"Where were you?" I asked later, unpacking the bags in the kitchen.

I was told to sit down. My mother crouched and shoved cans into cupboards, metal clanging against metal, as if she wanted me to hear the inside of her head.

On the next day, dust flew across the road and blinded anyone in the crescent. Kevin, Marty and I tried to play hockey: one boy went in goal while the others stood far back and drilled slapshots at him. After ten minutes we quit—we couldn't see. My stick on my shoulder, I shuffled home and found my mother on her knees, weeding the front yard flowerbed. Hair hidden under a straw hat, sleeves rolled up high, she jabbed the earth with a trowel. I turned around before she could hear me and give me a job. I hurried across the street, but didn't know where to go.

At the crescent's mouth, I reached Marty's house. A curtain moved in an upstairs window. I saw no-one, inside or outside, or anywhere else on the street. A gull squawked overhead. The wind had stopped. I sweated on the sidewalk, yet the whole crescent looked frozen: the solid, unflinching brick homes; the flat green lawns; the glinting driveway cars; all the poplars and their sword shadows.

I knocked on Marty's door and his father waved me inside.

In the kitchen the bald man stood and blinked, blue eyes buried in red skin.

"Martin's upstairs doing his German homework. *Schaffe schaffe*," smiled the father, black grease splotching his hands. *Schaffe schaffe*: work work. My mother talked like that.

"Can I get him?" I said.

"Sit."

He poured me a glass of milk, then his hands flickered over the table and he picked up a metal disc. It belonged to the blender lying in pieces on newspaper. He talked to me for a long time about how to repair it, but the details confused me. I sipped my milk and nodded.

He coughed, wiped his hands with a rag. "Any news about your dad?"

I said nothing.

"Walter, you don't know what it was like in 1951, when he came here. *I know*. You show up, you get a room, you get a job, then someone hears you speak German and—"

"Hi!"

Marty's blond hair stood straight up. He walked into the kitchen and smiled. The phone rang. I listened to his father talk about me in German.

Marty came to my side. "Maybe we can go—"

"No," snapped his father. "Sorry." He added what I'd already guessed: my mother wanted to see me right away. Head down, I left my friend.

At home I let the screen-door slam behind me. I smelled hairspray. My mother rushed up and smeared a fistful of Bryl-creem into my hair, flattening it and making my head stink. I turned away but she took my arm and jerked me into the hall.

I stopped breathing. I didn't want to smell myself—or her. Her hair, lipstick, shoe polish.

"Go upstairs," she said. "Put on a white dress shirt and your good brown pants. We have company. Don't forget your belt. Then come downstairs and wait in the living-room. Reporters from *The Toronto Star* are here." Her grip on my arm tightened. "Just say Daddy drowned."

I'd already heard the men in our kitchen. I walked heavily up the stairs until I heard the kitchen door close. I turned, tiptoed back down and sat on the second-lowest step. I'd change my clothes later. Now, despite the shut door, I could easily hear the male voices, along with my mother's. I always heard it. Even when I slept.

"I do everything myself," she whined. "This morning I rewired the toaster. And the pear tree, the plum tree, the garden, the berries, cutting the lawn. There's *so* much work."

"Mrs. Schwende, did your husband act at all strangely in his last weeks?"

She started sniffling.

"Franz always came home right from work," she whimpered. "And he always, *always* played with Walter. Last week Franz...."

"Mrs. Schwende," said another man's voice. "Do you think he'll come home?"

I could hear my mother crying.

"How was Franz's business doing?" said the first voice. "The window-framing shop in Unionville."

She didn't answer, and I wondered whether one of the men would rub her arm, the way my father did when she was upset.

The door flew open and I looked up at a huge man, his hair black and falling down over his collar.

"Walter the spy," he said. "Are you helping your mother as much as you can?"

"Yes."

He smiled and asked about the bathroom, so I led him upstairs. Just before he opened the door, I breathed in his cologne.

"Sir, do you know where my father is?"

He held the door and looked downstairs. After he heard voices, his eyes fixed on mine.

"The police dredged the harbour," he shrugged. "Nothing."

He was staring at me with his large brown eyes. When he turned, I tugged his sleeve. I wanted to talk more, to just stand beside him, but I didn't know what to say. He was an adult. Adults were always busy.

He squeezed my shoulder. "You're the man now."

"What does that mean?"

His lips quivered, but he didn't speak.

In 1973 I was a tall skinny fourteen-year-old with blue eyes, curly brown hair, and a slouching walk. That summer I went with my mother to a picnic near Uxbridge, on a large swath of parkland owned by the German church in Toronto. Dozens of German and Austrian families lounged on blankets, while barbeques sent the aromas of chicken, steak and sausage into the air. Children shouted and raced and fell in the grass. An enormous sunken concrete pool lay in the park's centre. Instead of swimming, I skulked about, ending up far from my mother. I stood with a plate of food beside my Uncle Karl, sprawled in a lawn chair. He was the husband of my mother's sister and our only male relative in Canada. Chicken grease and potato salad smeared his mouth; brown beer bottles lay in the grass under his chair. My Aunt Friedl sat beside him, eating a drumstick.

Adults made me nervous. Still, I smiled at my uncle.

His face red and puffy, his mouth full and his jaws chewing loudly, he could only wink back. I remembered his dog.

"Uncle Karl, did you bring Fritzie?"

His throat moved, and I imagined the wad of mushed chicken and potato sliding downward. He reached for his beer.

"Not today, Walter," he said, and winked again. "I brought my wife."

Aunt Friedl gave a sharp laugh, like she was just able to stop herself from choking. Why didn't she say something?

She did get off her lawn chair and walk away, but I was distracted by the shouts and splashes coming from the pool. A young girl emerged, her hands going up the top rungs of the poolside stairs. Droplets shone on her skin, and I stared until I heard my uncle's voice.

"Where's your dad?"

Uncle Karl was eating again: another drumstick half-disappeared into his mouth.

I wanted to rip that drumstick out and punch his face as hard as I could. Just like I wanted to lift up the end of his chair and spill his fat disgusting body into the grass. But he was gigantic—he'd strangle me.

"What a *stupid* thing to say," I spat. My face burned. I'd never spoken like that to an adult.

"Uncle Karl, he's been dead for seven years."

My uncle reached over to the cooler, took out a beer and used his belt buckle to uncap it. He gave it to me.

"You really think so?" he smiled.

I sat at his feet, my first beer in hand, my mouth open.

When you disappear, for the longest time no-one knows you have. There's only a quietness that grows in the person left behind, that fills the body with air. You have taken the other's insides and replaced them with an airy nothing, a hollow. The left-behind person becomes something suspended, like a winter leaf rattled by wind. Still, the hollow must be filled. Quickly. The person left behind will fill it with anything: memories strong and weak, guesses, rumours, other people's stories. He can substitute what he wants to recall for what he can't, or for whatever happened that he didn't like. Or that embarrassed him. All that matters is filling the hole.

I sit here at my desk, lights like tiny moons suspended in the window. Amid the moons appear my face and torso, the ruffled brown hair and hunched shoulders. I look at my reflection and picture Franz Schwende's escape, the first eastward flight, an all-night drive after he left us. Yes, I can imagine it: my father getting into a car and driving, just like we did on our day trips together. But now he's alone.

The night sky breaks apart, everything goes dim. The clouds are blue and indigo. He drives a '61 Plymouth down the riverside highway into a full-on assault, the rain detonating against the windshield as if the sky wants to drown him. Wipers flicked on, he slows his speed yet welcomes the rain as a good omen, its pounding of his roof like the blood pulsing in his head. And thunder cracks, white light fissures the horizon. He drives into a long curve greased by rain. His car begins to drift, to slide sideways, to spin in circles. He grips the steering-wheel harder, squints at the brush and rocks revolving outside his window. Twenty-four hours ago in Toronto, he left us—his wife and son—and now he wonders how he'll be received in Montreal. On he spins, a one-ton metal top. He sees the curve end and glances down at his turquoise Hawaiian shirt, its festoon of straw-skirted maidens and airborne sharks. When he looks up, the front of his car hits a willow and stops dead.

Rain machine-guns the roof.

No cars, no-one heading east or west.

Blown riverward, a gull eyes the crash and looks away, not even bothering to squawk at the weather.

Steam curls from the crumpled hood, tangles with the rain and vanishes. The motor has stopped. He turns the ignition key back and forth. Not a click.

He keeps his eyes open. Moves his arms, his legs. He leans forward, lifts the bottle from his crotch and tips the bottom straight up, drinks what beer is left and swears: *Verdammtes Wetter*. He puts his horn-rimmed glasses in their case and uses his shirt to wipe down the wheel and cigarette lighter and door handle, which he pushes open. Outside, he flings the bottle into the river and confronts his car, knows it's scrapyard-bound and he'll get nothing: he can't stay. The day before—after dumping the family Volkswagen near the racetrack—he bought the Plymouth off a used lot for $1000. Half his money. He peels the temporary licence off the inside rear window, folds it into a tight square, slips it in his pocket. A canvas bag hooked over his shoulder, he shuts the door with his hip and crosses the road. Shirt, shorts, socks, sandals already drenched, he heads into the wind and rain, toward the last large town.

He jogs, walks, jogs again, and soon he's put a mile between himself and the wreck. No vehicle approaches in either direction, but his watch says it's 6.30 and on this summer morning, only people travelling to work would risk the storm. He continues along the highway shoulder, a big man, 6'1" and 180 pounds. Walking through the rain, he smells the sweat-stink that seeps through his clothes. He stops and spits. He owes $60,000 and can't go home—not now, maybe never. Even if he gets to Montreal and is given refuge, he has no notion of where to go next. Now he stands completely still, his shirt shivering his skin. He wonders whether another omen exists, a simple hint of what to do. Blurred slants of rain rip up puddles; a barn roof gapes; and far above the river an arched, half-fogged span ferries traffic to and from America. When a car crawls by in the opposite lane he averts his face, forces himself to stare at the sumac, its undergrowth, the place where dead and living things are dry.

My father walks on, passes a rusted truss bridge and a boat launch, the masts tipping back and forward like timid punches.

# 2. Mission

In the fall of '84 I thumbed across the country to Vancouver and soon ran out of money. I thought my university friends—the guys I'd lived and partied with for the last year—would send the money they owed me. Nope. So, my funds almost gone, I moved into the basement of a West End rooming-house, a two-storey building brimming with men on welfare. For a while I tried to find work, then I listened to my new housemates and learned their tricks. At the end of the next month, I too started to get those nice thick brown envelopes.

One night I heard a familiar knock on my door.

"It's open."

A small man in a T-shirt stuck his head in. Anton. He and another Czech named Jan lived above me. They were New World bachelors: young refugees whose wives had left them as soon as they reached Canada. A same-old same-old story for them, but one I hadn't known.

A lock of black hair swished across Anton's face. I stared at his platform shoes.

"Walter, why about women are you so naïve?"

I held out my hands. "If I knew why I was so naïve, I would not be so naïve."

Anton's smile revealed gold teeth. "Now you are sophist. But come. Let's go Burger King."

At the restaurant we always sat with our backs to the wall. Anton called it Gary Cooper's law, but his main reason for sitting this way—and sipping styrofoam coffee for hours— was his art. Plus a wish to seduce. He would prop his sketchpad against our table, flip to a fresh page, ready his pencil and scan the room for a subject. His preferred model was a woman sitting alone, and he tried to work fast so he could hand her the portrait before she left. He admitted that this ploy had never brought him a date, let alone sex, but some of the women nodded when they saw him again and once a woman bought him a coffee.

Today was like every day. We sat and drank as Anton's left hand arced and shaded.

"Walter, you are a good-looking guy. Tall, blue eyes, nice skin. Tell me, how do you approach Canadian women?"

"That's a good question."

"In my country, sleeping with someone is just finish of good talk. But the women here, they are cold. Maybe is rain, maybe the British influence in your country. I'm not sure. Even the women in street don't look at you, but at home everyone look, stare, smile, even look angry. At least something. The only women here who smile at me are Burger King women."

"They have to smile."

"Cannot be true, Walter. Even in a Communist country they cannot make you smile, unless with torture."

We had discussed the cashiers' smiles before but I could never convince Anton that, to use his favourite taunt, he was being naïve.

Jan came through the door and winked at us, then he went off to order a coffee. At our table, he sat down and pulled a manila envelope from his satchel. Using an elastic band, he gathered his brown hair into a ponytail.

Jan spread out his sheaf of shiny 8-by-10 black-and-white photographs. I put down my cup. Anton smiled.

I was looking at three different versions of the same shot: a rose nestled in female pubic hair.

Jan grinned. "Pussy pin-ups."

"All the same girl?" I said.

"Yes. In summer I went to Wreck Beach with camera. I tell women I am a visiting artist, and women interested. Sometimes I take a beach shot in sand, but always I suggest a special photo in studio. Lily say yes."

"Did you sleep with her?"

Anton laughed. "Walter, you like this question."

26

Jan shrugged. "No, though she is posing with many photos. But that's not best."

"What's best?" I said.

Jan glanced away, then looked at me.

"She let me put rose in."

I studied his face, the droopy brown eyes and scruffy beard.

Anton closed his sketchpad and clapped his hands.

"Let's go strip bar!"

None of us had much money, but at least once a week we left the house together and did something. Sometimes we'd walk down to the Czech café on Denman and sit with our elbows on the red-and-white tablecloths, and I'd watch Anton and Jan eavesdrop on the Czech conversations at other tables, all the talks between men whose heads were bent close together. I'd see women, but rarely and never alone. But the men— once, when my friends and I had traded the warm café for the drizzle outside, I'd asked about what they'd heard. Nothing, they said, glaring at me. Anton shrugged and told me it was the same talk he bored me with: the wife, the horrible beer, the life here.

Sometime in February, in what was still called winter by locals—though it was ten degrees Celsius—Jan stood with us on the wooden floor of our rooming-house lobby. He suggested a thrift-store trip. He said he needed new shirts, for he'd thrown out the ones that were torn or faded. A few minutes later, Anton and I waited for him on the sidewalk, and I heard that Jan's real reason for wanting new shirts was the source of the old ones: his wife had bought them when she and Jan arrived in Vancouver. Anton said the shirts were actually in good condition, they just brought Jan bad memories.

He came bounding out of the house. I smiled. His eyes were either half-closed or bugging out at you, as if accusing you of being too lazy and apathetic to realize that life was dancing all around.

"Walter, you're like an old man—" Jan grabbed my shoulders and straightened them "—you must stand like soldier. Did you forget where we're going?"

"No, but—"

Jan circled me, rubbing his jaw.

"Salvation Army!" he said. "Hut—hut—hut!"

We walked side-by-side down the streets between Robson and Davie, and I'd often drop back to let an oncomer pass. Anton and Jan would scold me for being a typical Canadian, always willing to give in. I didn't bother to argue, but I still gave people the room they needed. I also watched the gait of my friends.

Jan walked with his shoulders back and chest out, like the martinet he wanted me to be. Anton stooped. He kept looking at the grass and sidewalk for money. Still, he was distinctive: with his high cheekbones and flapping black forelock, his green velour shirt and bell-bottoms and three-inch heels, he looked like a seventies disco guy. People stared, and he liked that.

"Paradise!" said Jan, as we passed through the glass doors of the Sally Ann.

Women in red smocks stood behind cash registers and ministered to the patrons: leather-jacketed punks in tight jeans and black running-shoes; grim-faced men and women, their hair straggly or long and feathered; Chinese and East Indian women, wheeling their carts down the aisles. My friends and I went in separate directions: they went for shirts and I for books.

I spent some time looking at paperbacks with garish spines, at hardcovers with titles like *Maybe I'm Dead*.

"Walter—" Anton had come up behind me "—you should borrow my books for free. You have read *Exile and the Kingdom*? *The Iceman Cometh*?"

"I've heard of them."

He grabbed my sleeve. "Let's rescue Jan. He has 23 shirts

and wants five."

Anton had a purple corduroy jacket hung over his arm, along with a wide yellow tie. He led me to Jan, who'd spread his potential purchases across the long rack of men's shirts.

"Walter," Jan said, "your country is impossible."

I looked at him.

"Choice!" he said. "Just too much." He held up a red, a blue, and a white shirt. "Czech colours," he smirked. "But who cares. How do I know what Canadian woman wants?"

"*A* Canadian woman," corrected Anton. "You are forgetting the indefinite article."

"You are forgetting you're stupid," said Jan, and turned to me.

"I'm serious, Walter. You must help me—do I buy five red, five blue or five white? Red is love, I know. Blue makes me look intellectual, and white is a nice contrast with my brown eyes and hair. So tell me—which one?"

Anton said: "You are forgetting the most important thing."

Jan thrust his chin forward.

"I'm sorry," said Anton, "but your face. Your twisted nose and little eyes. Like Frankenstein's monster, but worse. Of course, maybe you'll get pity-love—"

Jan took five white shirts and left all the others splayed on the rack. I resisted the urge to hang them back up with their corresponding colours.

"Let's go home," said Jan, his shirts against his chest. "White is the best choice—because I am pure and beautiful."

Spring arrived, but the pink plum and cherry blossoms didn't make me feel any more alive. I went to bed at four each morning and slept till noon, then took a nap after supper. Sometimes I jogged around the sea wall, wrote letters or visited my friends. I witnessed the eventual growth of breasts on a tall man who walked up and down Davie Street. I also read novels and the occasional newspaper. Reagan was meddling in Central America. The paper piled the bad news into a neat little stack with a fold down the middle. Just reading it gave you a luxurious warm-bath feeling, one that changed nothing.

One night I finished a run and walked the last block to my room. The side streets were empty, the air smelled of wet grass. I was tired, but at peace. Running always let me clear my head, relax, even daydream. And I liked to be between places, especially outside.

In my room, I stepped on a scrap of paper.

*Walter, I have news. Come see me.*

Anton often left me notes, telling me to meet him in his room, at Burger King, or on a bench by the Lost Lagoon snack bar in Stanley Park.

The door to his first-floor room was open. Anton's place was three times larger than mine and wooden sculptures littered the mantelpiece, bookcase, window-sill, even the floor. On his table stood a thin nine-inch figure. I picked it up, and noticed how the grooves in the folds of a cloak were burnt dark and the entire sculpture was made of one piece of light-coloured wood. The top third wasn't finished. I looked at Anton, who had a small block of wood in his hand.

"What's going on?" I said.

He dropped the wood on the window ledge and it made a knocking sound.

"Jan moved. He has a job." Anton nodded. "He is the assistant manager of a building. He is working weekends and getting free place."

"What does he do?"

"He is showing people apartments." Anton smiled. "Jan is like a tour guide. And you know who he is meeting."

I couldn't tell if Anton's head was nodding or shaking—if he was proud of his friend, or jealous.

Jan's new place was located on the seventh floor of a nine-storey building. He let us into the apartment and I glanced at the fridge, stove, bed, empty pizza boxes, phone, guitar against the wall and stuffed hockey bag in the corner. No couch, table or chairs.

Jan handed me a cold beer.

"Walter, there is princess in 506."

He started hopping from one foot to the other, shouting "506! 506!" and Anton walked into the room carrying three more beers by their necks.

"Who is she?" I said.

"Forty-year-old secretary with red hair. Tomorrow I will visit her for supper. And she is telling me she love making pasta!"

We sat and drank beer on Jan's floor while he played guitar, his fingers flying over the strings. He sang "My Brown Pimpled Girl," a song he'd written about a Hastings Street drug addict. Jan did a song in Czech, and he played "Imagine." Later he went into the kitchen and came back with a plate of tuna flakes on crackers. We ate the food and drank more beer, and whenever Jan shouted "506! 506!" Anton and I would smile and clink his bottle. Eventually, though, his shoulders slumped, and when Anton tried to hand him another beer he shoved it away.

"There is a problem," Jan said, his eyes wet. "I have girl-friend."

I glanced at Anton, who was studying a brown blotch on the ceiling.

"I do not understand," Jan said. "My first day we meet in the office and that night she sleep with me. It's nice, then she tells me she has husband and son in Montreal. One month ago she just left family and came to Vancouver, like it is nothing." Jan looked at me. "Walter, it's against nature."

Anton also looked at me. Each man's eyes were narrow, accusatory.

"What do you want?" I said to Jan, then a hole opened up in my stomach.

Anton and Jan traded looks and shook their heads from left to right, hair falling into their faces.

Walking home, Anton stopped me under a streetlamp.

31

His stubbled cheeks were sucked in.

"Walter, this question was wrong question. You know what we want. We want wives back. But is not possible." Anton spread out his arms. "So we do not know what we want. So everything is pretend."

After seven months of rooming-house life I was tired of it. Not tired of Anton and Jan, just tired. In May I answered an ad for a security-guard job up north, and three days later I got it.

I had to say goodbye.

In his room Anton sat in a chair by the window, reading the back pages of a magazine splayed open on his lap. *Psychology Today*. He looked especially thin.

"Walter, you can get a wife. Columbian, Filipino—I counted 40 names and addresses."

"Even if you get them from a catalogue, you still need money to keep them."

Anton frowned. "Money is not problem. I can get a job. More important, I know what a woman wants. Spontaneous guy. But a woman wants to feel safe too. You make them laugh, feel like queen, fuck them of course—and once a month you give rose." Anton winked. He stood and did a little dance, the sides of his shirt collar flopping like wings ready to lift him to the ceiling. Still, his glibness bothered me.

"Why did your wife leave you?" I said.

He looked at me when he spoke, and pushed his forelock out of his face.

"More than a year ago we came here, at the start of winter. Magda and me do not speak English, I do not get job—I am like a child in your country. Walter, you must understand. Back home, maybe the woman works in shop, factory, office, but then she comes home and cooks and makes self look good for her man. The man comes home from job, there is food, maybe sex, and at night they go to bar. But the woman does

32

what the man says—is not even question. Then we come to your country and everything is upside down. Everything is fear. The woman is worried because the husband cannot get job. And apartment, food, even beer is expensive. The man is getting depressed and the woman is becoming more afraid. So Canada is like prison." Anton held out his palms, as if to prove he was hiding nothing.

"Then some Slav guy who came to Canada five, ten years before, he meets the man's wife and makes good impression. It's happening many times. It happened to me."

And to Jan, I thought, and watched Anton push back his forelock.

"I had a friend," he said. "Leo is road engineer in Prague and welfare guy here, like me. He tells me after his first week in Canada, 'Anton, I find freedom.' But he cannot get job, and after a year his wife goes with Polish doctor. Two months after she leaves, Leo jumps from building roof. His blood goes all over parked car. People find him on the sidewalk."

Anton pointed a finger at my face.

"Just imagine, Walter. In Communist country, man and woman escape together. In West, woman escapes man, then man escapes life. It's crazy."

His cheeks pulsed, and I thought about how rarely I saw him calm.

"Anton, when did Magda leave?"

"In July. I am away for summer."

"Doing what?"

He put a hand on his hip. "One day I will show you."

"I got a job up north. I'm leaving in three days."

He looked at me.

"What you are doing tomorrow?"

"Packing."

"I will make the phone call. If everything is okay, we take bus."

"Where?"

"We go Mission."

"On a mission?"

"No. Mission is the name of town."

"But why are we going?"

Anton tilted his head. "It's pilgrimage."

From his table, he picked up the sculpture I'd seen before and passed it to me. Though less than a foot high it felt heavy, solid. The top folds of a woman's cloak became hands covering her downcast face.

"It's called 'Daughter of Christ,'" Anton said. Noticing my frown, he added: "Because even this guy needs a woman." Anton grinned. "I finished sculpture this morning and you got a job. So tonight we go strip club, tomorrow we go Mission."

The bus left the station early and I slept until we reached the town. Anton led me along streets of one- and two-storey buildings to a church made of brown brick. The front doors were open. After the glare of sunlight the interior light seemed thick, soupy. We waded through it on our walk up the nave. Anton stopped at the altar and I stared at the crucifix on the wall, a ten-foot-high Christ looming above us.

"White pine, Walter. It's a three-month job, fifteen hours each day. I start at seven, am covered in sawdust and woodchips till late at night. The priest says, 'Anton, you work too hard, have some beer before bed.' I tell him, 'Father, in this time I drink the pain of Christ. I not need beer.'"

"How did you make it?" I said.

"I use no electric tools, just hand. And the chisel, knives, these kinds of things. Some parts of the body need deep grooves, even hollow like hole. I try to make what is called *jednota*. Unity. Look how the arms, hands, eyes, mouth are all open. Walter, I am lucky. In your country you have wood with straight grain. I work with the grain, not against. Is like relationship."

He said it like it was simple, obvious, and I tried to take it like that. I looked away, concentrating on the long stretch of pews, the candles flickering against a wall.

Anton coughed, and the sound echoed in the church.

"So Walter, I finish job. I go home with one thousand dollars in pocket. The apartment is empty—just note. I do not even want to get drunk. And I decide suicide is stupid. I am 30-year-old guy who just made Christ."

That night we stayed in the rectory with the grey-haired priest and drank his beer as we swapped hitch-hiking stories. In the morning Anton and I returned to Vancouver, and though I planned on going to bed early, he insisted on one last walk.

The evening was cool and full of gulls. Anton led the way along Denman, past cafés and a glass-walled tavern. We cut over to the concrete path that followed the sea wall around Stanley Park. Runners, cyclists, men and women pushing baby carriages, other walkers: the human stream flowed around us.

As we passed a beach, Anton stopped, forcing people to veer or also stop.

"Walter, are you a determinist or believer in free will?"

"Free will, I guess."

"Of course. And in Communist country, for this they would jail you."

"I don't understand."

He started to walk quickly, his forelock swinging across his face, his untucked shirt billowing behind him. I tried to keep up.

"In my country," he said, looking straight ahead, "is against law to not have job. You cannot be artist. Everyone must be producing for the State. One time I was construction worker—*me*! Anyway, other workers and me, including Jan, we are starting drinking at lunch. The boss is begging us to come back to job. He buy everyone three half-litres of beer if we promise to go back."

"Pretty funny," I said.

"It's not funny. It's Communist system. They want you to love job, to love state, more than wife, friends, your own parents. Walter, you are spontaneous guy, hitch-hike across country. In my country they say to you, 'Okay Walter, be spontaneous guy in jail. Walk around cell on your hands.'"

Anton put his arm around me. We watched a white sail-boat, its dip and lift in the waves.

"Walter, sometimes I am thinking about you like brother. But there is problem. You are kind of Western guy Lenin called 'useful idiot.'"

On the next day I flew to Watson Lake and bussed to the mining town of Clayton. For months I patrolled the mill-site with my walkie-talkie, listening to ravens caw. I also read the newspaper whenever it showed up. Reagan's support of mercenaries in Nicaragua hadn't stopped. I wanted to go there, to work as a volunteer. I wrote Anton a long letter, explaining why my Communists were good Communists. He replied immediately: a postcard of a Mountie in a red tunic. On the card's back, he had printed my address and just two words: *Walter* and *Anton*. There was a wide space between our names.

# 3. Down Time

"The fucking fucker's fucked."

"Excuse me?"

"The tramline motor. It quit twenty minutes ago."

Grey light pressed against the window as talk stopped at other tables in the mess, where coveralled men bent their heads over breakfast. I went quiet too because I feared asking the man a stupid question. Instead I watched him put his hardhat and styrofoam cup on my table, then wipe his brow with the sleeve of his coveralls. Grease smeared his forehead. Long, flat, black hair made his whole head seem oiled. Blinking sweat from his eyes, he looked half-human, half engine-part.

"You're the new hire," he said, eyeing my silver earrings. "Security."

"I'm waiting for Bren O'Hearne."

The man scowled and ripped off part of his cup's lid.

"That Newfie prick stole my girl." The man pointed behind me. "Belly—that's her behind the counter."

I turned but couldn't see a woman. Though I remembered one.

"Is he still with her?" I said.

"Nope. She even came crawling back to me, but I wouldn't take her. You need some pride in this hole."

The man tore open three packets from the table bowl and dumped the sugar into his coffee. He muttered something.

"Down time," he said, louder. "We don't fix that motor by noon, they'll be sending men home for sure."

"Do they still get paid?"

"First five days. Don't know if that applies to you though." The man slurped his coffee. "Your boss might need you in case things get weird. Fights, B&Es, sabotage. Or he might just send you back to where you're from."

The man's mouth twitched at the sound of footsteps. After

a glance behind him, he picked up his hardhat and left.

"Walter Schwende?" A tall man with blue eyes sat down. A moustache and sunburnt cheeks gave him a cowboyish look. His eyes travelled from my earrings to the men at other tables, their forks moving up and down. A few men glanced our way.

"I bet Fratzie had some choice words for me."

"If you're Bren, one or two."

Bren shook his head. "That's the town of Clayton right there. I'll be glad to get out."

"You're leaving?"

"In about 356 hours—not that I'm counting." Bren spread his hands and tapped the table. "Guess you flew into Watson Lake last night. Where you from—Vancouver?"

"I came here from there, but I'm from Toronto. Scarborough, actually." I picked at my plate of cold eggs.

"An Upper Canadian," Bren said. He stuck out his hand. "Welcome."

His palm was clammy.

Bren was rubbing the crowned heart tattoo on his arm when a female voice ignited laughter nearby. The woman who'd served me walked toward us, trays stacked in her arms. Fratzie's stolen ex.

"How are ya, Belly?" Bren said.

"Better than most—as you know." She looked me over. "You're the new S/G."

I read the lettering on her baseball cap: *Sahara Marina.*

"I wear it for the subtle man," she winked, and walked off.

Bren thrust a thumb in her direction. "That woman can do things with six inches of cock that a monkey couldn't do with 40 foot of rope."

I pushed aside my plate. Bren stared at the bread crusts and bacon fat.

"Any women here my age?" I asked, scanning the room. Beyond the window the grey light had thinned, revealing the shapes of trees and shingled buildings.

Bren looked at me. "Sprightly things are rare. So are single ladies. We've got seven. But you better be careful. Around here, there's a lot of scuffling for a honey. Just last week some hardhat shot a guy in the stomach for taking his girl."

"But did she willingly go with the guy?"

"That doesn't matter."

We walked along a gravel road that curved toward the town limits, and at the rec centre we met a crew sodding the front lawn. Bren introduced me to Stacey, a native girl with short hair, a purple halter-top and a space between her front teeth. She stopped rolling out sections of grass to stare at me and smile.

As Bren and I neared the mill-site, large glossy ravens lifted and fell around us, their caws and thuffs seeming to deepen the creases in Bren's face. Pickup wheels rumbled and engines revved in the distance. An eighteen-wheel truck rattled past the security gate and toward the road out of town. The driver shouted Bren's name, then drew a hand across his neck. I looked at Bren but he glanced away, fixed his eyes on the smoke rising from a mill-site building, the white plumes twisting into a sky of washed-out blue.

A short man stood between the hut and the security gate. He looked like authority: the epauletted shirt and creased pants, the side-parted grey hair, the eyes brown and dull.

Bren spoke. "Ron Tenet, Walter Schwende. Our new S/G."

Ron raked his eyes over me. "You're a day late."

"In Vancouver they said to report for work on 27 May."

"I'll try to forget your first mistake, Mr. Schwende. But I'm wondering one thing—why here? You could get beat up back East just as easy."

Bren led me away after telling Ron we'd be touring the mill-site.

Clumps of pale green asbestos stuck to our boots as we walked between long buildings with ribbed roofs. When workers saw Bren, most looked away.

"Welcome to Pleasantville," he said.

"What makes Ron like that?"

Bren nudged me with an elbow. "Look around."

Lunch buckets in hand, men streamed out of buildings and pulled off their hardhats, some men flinging them onto the ground. At least 200 workers converged on the security gate and the road to town. Down time: for now, work was over. No-one looked our way, though I saw some empty stares and wet cheeks, heard men swear at the ground or each other. I turned to Bren. I didn't understand the grin on his face, the ends of his mouth tugged upward as if he couldn't control them.

Some time after lunch, a knock on my bunkhouse door startled me. I opened the door to Bren. He stood there in a plaid shirt with rolled-up sleeves, his right-hand dangling a six-pack of Kokanee. He gaped at my hair.

"I should've warned you."

I hadn't seen him since our morning tour of the mill-site. He'd dropped me off at the security hut, where Ron proceeded to overwhelm me: first with the reek of his aftershave lotion, then with details. He showed me how to write reports, man the gate, work the walkie-talkie, use the time-clock and logbook. He stressed the need to check the backs of trucks for fresh kill, moose or caribou. Poachers hid them under tarps and blankets. Also, poachers had to use the security gate because it blocked the sole access to a valley owned by the mine. I had to be especially cautious now: less work activity meant fewer people around, and poachers would feel bold. My job was to log all details of an encounter with a poacher and immediately notify Bren, the security-company adjutant. Ron added that I should never try to apprehend someone. Pushing up his sleeves, he held out forearms full of crooked scars. *Knife fights*, he said, *from the good old days*. Ron made me take out my earrings and then he sent me to Clayton's barber for a brush-cut. Now I looked

40

like an extra on "Happy Days."

Bren surveyed the pants and books on my floor, levered the caps off two beers with his belt buckle and handed one over.

"Lube up before your first shift."

Someone passed by the window, grinding the gravel.

"Well, just one," I said. "I don't want Ron smelling booze on my breath."

Bren sat in the only chair and drank. "Listen, don't go thinking we're *all* assholes."

"Hey," I laughed, "I attract abuse."

"Maybe. But people here need enemies. When you let a guy be different, it's like you don't have a stance worth defending. And if you don't mind me saying, you seem like a real city-type. We're not used to seeing guys with their ears pierced three times."

I lifted my shoulders and dropped them.

"Bren, Ron said you've worked in mines for 30 years. Twenty here. You must've seen a lot."

He held up his bottle. "A lot of these. And women even curvier."

He pulled a thick wad of bills from his pants pocket. After licking his fingertips, he made the money crack by rubbing each bill between his thumb and index finger. I saw browns and reds. Constantly wetting his fingers, the money just inches from his face, Bren counted his wad twice. When he finished his last count, he held aside a $100 bill and looked at me, then stuffed all his money back in his pocket.

"Soon," he smiled, "I'll be smacking my cash down on some realtor's desk. 50 Gs. All for a tidy little place back in God's country." Bren leaned toward me. "But I'm still five grand away from peace-of-mind. From security." He coughed, a harsh rasping sound that seemed to stay in the room. "That, sir, is the only reason I'm still here. Get some new business and collect some old debts."

I heard the bunkhouse door open and close.

"How old is Stacey?" I said.

Bren grinned. "Old enough. You know what they say—
'Fifteen'll get you twenty, but sixteen'll get you laid.'"

He looked at my face like he was trying to read it.

"She's a good girl though, that one. Plays on her school's
baseball team. Don't think she's ever had a boyfriend but I
wouldn't really know, there being about 35 years between
us."

"Bren—" I paused "—I'm worried about what'll happen
to me."

"You mean down time? Hey, they'll need security more
than ever. You'll be fine. Just stick with your buddy Bren."

"But you're leaving."

"Got to." Bren coughed, wiped his mouth with his fingers.
"Walter, look around. Behind almost everyone you see there's
a broken marriage, a broken country, a crime, a drug or
drinking problem. The North will let you hide and heal. At
first." Bren drank.

"Then suddenly you've got money and only your old
mistakes to spend it on. That's no fun. So you party, buy toys,
buy whores in Whitehorse, take fancy trips, run up crazy
debts on your credit card. You came to Clayton thinking
you'd stay just long enough to kill some debt and tuck away
some cash. Twenty years later you can't leave." Bren tipped
back the rest of his beer. "That was almost my story, till I
decided to turn things around." He patted his pocket.

"So you're going back to Newfoundland," I said. "Alone."

Smiling, Bren opened another beer. "A week or so trolling
the George Street bars in St. John's, and I'll secure a lady
willing to share my sheets." Bren drank. "Not a lot of options
back home, and I'll be the man with money, a house, and
endless charm and wit."

"All the charm and wit you learned here."

"Exactly."

Bren drained his second beer. He told me to meet him at
the security gate at three o'clock, an hour away. When he left
I lay on my bed and stared at the pine beams supporting the

roof. One beam had graffiti on it, but I was too tired to get up and look. Too tired yet too nervous. I tried not to think about my first shift. And I wondered about Bren. Why would he expose so much of himself to someone he hardly knew? Maybe it was because we had no history—with me, he could start all over. I knew the strategy.

An hour into my first shift I sat in the security hut and, shielding my eyes from the sun, gazed at the electronic accident-prevention board across the road. Apparently the warehouse had gone 3462 days without an "LTA"—a lost-time accident, Bren explained. At the bottom of the board, flanked by orange double-triangles, glared a warning:

REMEMBER
SAFETY IS A STATE OF MIND

For the next two hours Bren leaned against the filing cabinet while I answered the phone, manned the gate, and recorded the licence plates of eighteen vehicles in the logbook. Fratzie came through, nodding at me and throwing a slit-eyed look at Bren. I also met the tie-clad mine manager and mill superintendent. I didn't recognize their accents; Bren said they were South African. Later, when he was in the washroom, I lifted the gate and had a talk with a diesel mechanic. He told me the mechanics were *givin' 'er*, taking the entire tramline motor apart.

I returned to the hut and found Bren outside, staring at the sky. He coughed. Without turning, he told me to take my supper break.

On my return I picked up the time clock and walked the mill-site. Near the end of my inspection a sudden rain drenched me. Twenty minutes later the sun came out, its glow turning everything orange: the mill-site buildings, the jack pines, the distant rec centre and mess, the jagged mountains that circled the town like sentinels. Soon the sun fell from sight.

43

Bren was still on supper break and I was alone at the gate when the red pickup pulled up, a dark tarp covering a large object in the back. The driver rolled down his window and said he was a mine-site engineer. He politely asked me to open the gate so he and his partner could get to the mess before they closed the kitchen.

"I have to check your back," I said.

"Just drills and a pile of tramline cable under that there tarp. Give us a break, buddy. We're starving."

The passenger's face was turned away from me.

I was about to go to the gate when I noticed two rifle-butts sticking out from a blanket behind the cab's seat.

"Sorry," I said to the driver. "I have to check every truck."

Beneath the tarp was the flank of a huge, brown-skinned animal.

The door slammed; the driver stood beside me. He'd brought a waft of booze.

"Twelve-pointer. We've been tracking this bull since dawn. C'mon bud, make your life easy. You don't want to write a report. Just do us a favour and lift the gate."

The passenger came around to my side of the truck. He wore mirror-sunglasses, though there was hardly any light left in the day. Under the glare of the street lamp, he looked like a small-time hood.

"Hey Skinny, where's Bren?"

I looked at his sunglasses, saw my oversized hardhat and green coveralls, then I turned around and lifted the gate. The pickup sped off. In the hut, I recorded the licence-plate number and the departure time in my log, but nothing else. When Bren returned I told him what I'd seen and he apologized, said I shouldn't have to be put on the spot like that. He checked the logbook and wrote down what he said was the poacher's name. Bren told me he'd talk to Ron. He added that under no circumstances whatsoever should I tell anyone what had happened—including Ron.

Something was obviously up, but I kept quiet. At 10.45

the night-shift S/G arrived. As Bren and I walked under a starless sky back to the town-site, he told me I'd done well. He'd checked my patrol reports and the log. I looked forward to a beer with him in our bunkhouse TV-room.

One night later, Stacey showed up at my door. It was after midnight and I'd just returned from a snack at the mess.

She stood in my room and looked at the floor. She wore a Good Hope Lake baseball cap, jean jacket, and grey sweat pants stuffed into construction boots. Her left arm cradled the town's housewarming gift: a six-pack of Kokanee. She handed me a beer.

"I can't open it," I said.

She smiled slightly and bent down by the end of the bed. Lifting up the carpet, she withdrew an opener.

Stacey sat in the chair and I sat on the bed. I looked at her. I didn't know what to think—or say. I just stared and drank my beer, watching her drink hers. She didn't seem at all nervous. She sat there like a guy, legs wide apart and feet flat on the floor.

Finally I said, "What grade are you in?"

"Going into twelve."

I thought to myself, okay, she's seventeen or eighteen. Hopefully the latter.

"Are you *into* school?"

"I skip a lot." She downed the rest of her beer, opened another and passed me one, too.

I leaned forward. "You're not worried about failing?"

"They don't fail natives. People would call them racist. The principal would lose his job."

I scratched my head.

"Hey," she said. She got up and stretched, her hands reaching toward the ceiling beams. "Do you do massages?"

On each of the next five nights Stacey visited me, always around midnight. My room was at the end of the bunkhouse: she'd tap the corner of my window and I'd let her in the back door. We had to be quiet, which was easy in one way. She hardly spoke.

"Hear the rumour?"

It was a bright afternoon, my first day off after working six, and I was scuffling toward the town library when the truck stopped beside me. Its side-window framed the scruffy face of Fratzie, his eyes bulging as he waited for my response. He continued to wait.

It had happened four times: a pickup at the gate, Bren on supper break, and a driver telling me to not check his back. When one guy slipped me a white envelope and said give it to Bren, the obvious became even more so. Bren was making as much cash as possible before he went home, and I was his accomplice. Now I didn't know what to do. Unlike the other S/Gs, who seemed to have their own cliques, Bren had been kind to me since I arrived in Clayton. But maybe that was the point: he was buying me off.

"What's the rumour?" I said to Fratzie.

He'd heard that the mine's superintendents had flown to Vancouver to see the owners and recommend that the mine be permanently shut down. World asbestos prices had plummeted and the owners had mining options in Mexico, where labour costs were a third of Clayton's.

Fratzie shook his head, greasy locks swishing against his cheeks. "The bigwigs don't give one runny shit about us. Twelve hundred jobs. All the families. And a lot of guys are way too old to get work elsewhere." He spat in the road. "I was just at the mine-site—we still can't find the problem. And starting today we don't get paid." Fratzie stared at me, his eyes bloodshot. "The world just wants to fuck you."

I nudged his tire with my shoe and a pickup cruised by, Steve Miller's "Jet Airliner" blasting into the air, a dog sitting upright in the cab's front seat. The driver stuck his hand out the window and gave Fratzie the finger. He, in turn, honked his horn and smiled at me.

46

"So, shagged any of our women yet?"

I rested my arm on the cab's door. "Stacey Joseph."

Fratzie peered at my face. "Where'd you do her? The firebreak?"

"She comes to my room."

Looking past me, he whispered: "Home delivery."

"Every night."

Fratzie put the truck in gear and drove off toward his trailer at the end of town.

On my next shift, I was writing up my patrol report in the security hut when Bren called me outside.

"Check out the nightlife."

For once the sky wasn't clouded over. Streaks of green and yellow light zigzagged in a sky speckled by stars.

I went with Bren back into the hut and plugged in the kettle. He was examining the logbook when I spoke.

"What about the poaching, Bren?"

I had to say his name again before he turned.

"Walter, I know what's in your head. You see me breaking company rules. Lying. Listen, you've been here, what—a week? You're nowhere near figuring this place out."

The kettle whistled and Bren made us coffee. My job.

"But why poaching?" I said. "If the mine's higher-ups find out, won't they think we're a slack outfit and fire *all* of us? Eight guys would lose jobs because of you. Eight guys with the kinds of debts you've told me about."

Bren came up to me, his hands loose at his sides. He was smiling. "Tell me something, buddy. When Stacey's lying on her stomach and you're doin' her from behind, do you notice how the bear-tattoo on her left shoulder seems alive?"

Bren folded his arms across his chest and looked out at the accident-prevention sign.

The phone rang. A jubilant mine-manager told me the tramline motor was fixed—the mechanics spotted a sheared piece of metal and replaced it. When I told Bren, he swore and struck out at the desk, knocking his coffee all over my

47

report. On our walk back to the mess he asked me if I'd rat on him. I said no, but was glad the darkness hid the look on my face. In the mess he asked me again.

The firebreak cut a rocky swathe through the jack pines around the town-site, creating a jump supposedly too wide for flames to leap. Ever since a fellow S/G showed me this secluded path, and especially the high point from which you could view the mountains and mill-site, the tailings pile and town-site, I'd often come up here with my hand-sized cassette player and a Billy Bragg tape. Now I walked on the small rocks with Stacey. Our first outing, albeit one hidden from public view. S/Gs, according to Ron Tenet, shouldn't get friendly with the townspeople.

Stacey wore a pink tanktop and her baseball cap, along with jeans and a pair of Greb Kodiaks. Apart from a soft "hi" when we met, she hadn't spoken. We just moved down the firebreak, picking our steps carefully. It was mostly quiet: the trees seemed empty of ravens and chipmunks, and an electric saw buzzed in the town-site. Otherwise, the only sound came from our boots hitting the rocks.

"You drive a Cat?" Stacey said.

"A car and a van, but that's it." I didn't think she knew how to operate a backhoe, and I didn't understand why she'd asked the question.

"My dad drives a flatbed truck," she said, and palmed the sweat off her forehead. "He makes $175 a day. Pretty awesome, eh?"

I nodded. "You got your driver's licence?"

"Next year. But sometimes my brother lets me drive his truck, like when we go four-wheeling up in the mountains. That way he can ride shotgun and drink."

We were on the rise. The tailings pile rose in the distance, a 50-metre-high mound of ore detritus, full of flaky light-green stuff that sure looked like asbestos.

"We end up breathing that," I said.

48

"We'll all die soon," said Stacey. "Easterners first."

I laughed.

"Hey," I said, "do you talk much to Bren?"

She turned her back and began to walk in the direction we'd come from. When I caught up to her, she frowned at me.

"I've seen him french a dog. He's disgusting."

All the way back to the firebreak's start, Stacey didn't say a word. Before we went our separate ways, I stopped and took in her smooth face, her straight back. I touched her arm.

"Hey," she said. "I want to tell you a joke."

"Shoot."

"I forget."

She walked away.

A few hours later, on my afternoon shift, I watched Bren leave the hut for supper. He swung his hardhat back and forth as he walked. I still didn't know how he'd heard about Stacey. No way Fratzie would've told him. Did Bren arrange for Stacey to see me—another way to buy my silence? His influence was hard to imagine, given the firebreak talk she and I just had. I couldn't even believe that she'd spoken to him. On our walk she was the most talkative I'd seen, but in my room she hardly ever talked, despite the fact that we slept together every night. She didn't like questions. Whenever I asked about her family, her friends, the town itself, she just shrugged and took my hand, placing it where she wished. Stacey came to see me but I was always the guest, being taken where she wanted me to visit.

Loud honking announced the arrival of the fuel truck. The driver was my age. He had long sideburns and a diamond stud in each ear. He wore oil-splattered jeans and stank of gasoline. Tonight Fratzie sat with him in the cab.

"Wally boy," smiled the driver. "I hear your pujoginator's on night shift."

"Night wiggle," smirked Fratzie.

49

I laughed. People here spoke a different language.

"That Stacey Joseph," said the driver, "she goes like a skidoo without a kill switch."

Fratzie punched him in the shoulder. I raised the gate and they drove off, coughing exhaust behind them. It hung in the air, along with their laughter and talk. I kicked the base of the gate, denting it with my steel-toed boot.

I walked back to town after my shift and took little notice of the green and yellow lights dancing across the sky. I skipped my usual mess snack and went straight to my room. I tried to read but couldn't last beyond a paragraph. As I waited for Stacey, all I could think about was her slow, lazy movements—from door to chair to bed—and the smell of her sweat. Now I wondered whether it was just *her* sweat. And that night, for the first time in eight, she didn't show up. At five AM I was still lying awake on my bed, glancing every few minutes at the red-and-black face of my clock radio. At one point I stood up and read the graffiti scribbled on the ceiling-beam, presumably put there by a former S/G, maybe someone who had also known about the beer opener under the carpet.

*It doesn't kill you.*
*It doesn't make you stronger.*
*It's a waste of time.*

Saturday morning. Overcast. Ravens hopped on the roofs as I walked to the store in search of a *Globe and Mail*.

Today was Bren's last day in Clayton; tomorrow morning he'd be taking a bus to Watson Lake. And Stacey—she hadn't come to my room in five nights.

I waited for a pickup to pass me on the gravel road. The truck's stereo blared "Sweet Home Alabama" and the driver touched his baseball cap when he saw me. I went through the glass doors of the store, found a three-day-old *Globe* and lined up at the checkout counter behind a woman in a familiar jacket. She was putting groceries on the conveyor belt.

50

"Stacey."

She didn't flinch.

"Five bucks even," said the cashier, her lank hair falling over the front of her sweatshirt. She frowned at me and I wanted to scream.

I moved closer to Stacey as she shoved her groceries in a bag.

"Stacey," I said.

She turned around. I looked at the white T-shirt beneath her jacket, at her grey eyes.

"Sir, that'll be one dollar for *The Globe*."

I watched Stacey's back as she walked out of the store. I paid the cashier and went to the mess.

At the end of the long room, his back against the wall, Fratzie sat alone. He waved me over. I didn't see Bren. He was likely collecting envelopes, hustling from trailer to house to bunkhouse.

Fratzie's cheeks were pouched with food and he just nodded when I sat down with my tray. He wiped gravy and bits of steak off his plate with a slice of bread, moving it in ever-smaller circles until the plate was spotless. He ate the bread and asked if I was going to The Spill—Clayton's bar— for Bren's going-away party.

"Ron said S/Gs shouldn't fraternize in the bar."

Fratzie burped. "Come tonight. It'll give you an edge." He winked. "You show up where you're not expected, people need time to react. If they know you're comin' they get their ammo all set, all ready to plug you."

I nodded and then ate while he drank his coffee and got a refill. When he sat back down I thought, to hell with it.

"Fratzie, do you know about Bren's poaching?"

"Of course."

"I thought you hated him."

Fratzie put down his cup. "What are you trying to do?" He shook his head. "One thing you don't do here is rat. Even if you rat on an asshole, people just peg *you* for a rat." Fratzie drained his cup. "Walter, people here run rats out of town, or stomp them till blood comes out their ears."

I leaned over the table and hissed: "Then why does everyone here keep telling *me* stuff? Including you?"

He pushed his face close to mine.

"Around here, blabbing's like breathing. That's why most people are so messed up. They come here messed up, and get worse." Fratzie stood. "So almost everyone's a rat, but they're all different sizes. And you can't see the smart ones."

I walked back to the bunkhouse to change into my coveralls. The sun laid down its heat and I was making the only noise around. The ravens just listened.

Right before Bren took his supper-break, he handed me a coffee and said: "I'm about to kill him. The bastard trailing me my whole time here."

I was suddenly afraid—for Fratzie.

Bren pulled out his wad of bills and performed his finger-lick ritual.

"Who's your enemy?" I said.

He smiled, put on his hardhat. At the door he paused but didn't turn. "Regret."

My shift was uneventful. No poachers, no white envelopes. At 11 PM Bren didn't want to walk back to the mess together, but he promised to meet me later at The Spill. He had to talk to the night-shift S/G.

In my room I listened to pickup doors slam, one after another. Men and women were arriving at the bar after short drives from their homes, trailers, bunkhouse digs. I heard voices and laughter: the bar was filling up. People were primed to party, and all I could do was lie in my bed and wonder whether Stacey would be there. Impossible.

I put in my earrings, grabbed my Doc Marten boots.

When I entered The Spill, the smoke made me cough. I edged past a dance floor surrounded by clumps of men clutching drinks, and at the bar I found a banner draped under the counter: A SHOTGUN PATROLS THIS BAR ONE NIGHT A WEEK. YOU GUESS WHICH NIGHT.

I bought a beer and stood against a wall, at the edge of shouts, clinking bottles and power-chord rock. I stared at the heads of unknown men and women, some covered by baseball caps and cowboy hats. After four beers I was still alone, elbows poking me as talk of the mine wafted my way. I looked at the door and wondered about Bren. He never showed up, nor did I see anyone else I knew. I drank until last call.

As I was squeezing past the puddled tables on my way out, a hand fell on my shoulder. A tall man slipped a beer into my hand. I recognized him: a poacher.

"You on afternoons next week?"

"Yes."

"Should I give *you* the envelope?"

I looked at him. I shook my head.

The man grabbed the front of my shirt. "What do I do now?" he said, his mouth hanging open. I said nothing and finally he let go and drifted away, back into the groups of people splayed out beside their tables.

I went after him. When I pulled hard on his shoulder he turned around, his fist cocked.

I spoke into his right ear. "I'll take it."

I walked back to the bunkhouse in the dark. Six cans of beer were taped to my door and behind them was a thank-you note from Bren. I went down to his room and found it empty. I tried our TV-room. A new poster announced a town meeting next Friday in the rec centre. The mine's owners wanted to talk to workers and their families. Someone with a black marker had written *Ghost Town* across the poster's bottom. Someone else, in a red, smaller script, had scrawled *Get Out Now.*

# 4. So Long Ago It's Not True

Her note lay on the table. *Eat all the food that's in the pan. I went shopping. Don't go out. There's something important to tell you. Love Mom.* The note was likely weeks old and had been left whenever she went out, just as the food had been made daily and later eaten by her when I failed to appear. I held up the note. She had pressed heavily with her pencil, as if the thick lines of the message would ensure its commands were obeyed. I wasn't sure if the missing comma in *Love Mom* was intentional.

I walked down the hall toward my old room; her bedroom door gaped open. I smelled hairspray, perfume, starch. In the pebbled light, red and purple scarves hung from her mirror's frame, and on the dresser small bottles crowded a wooden box. Nestled inside were black-and-white photos I brought to the window's last light. There was a family portrait taken on my trip to Austria: a row of men in dark suits and women in floral dresses, their children clamped in place by hands on shoulders. In the foreground, a white-haired man sat and dandled a baby boy: my father's father and me. Behind us and separated by a thin space, my parents stood slightly sideways. The adult smiles could not hide the embarrassment of country people in a formal moment. I slid the photo beneath the others and thumbed through laughing girls clasping one another's waists. The last photo showed a young woman dancing past a sofa, her head tilted and black hair cascading behind her, her eyes and mouth shut, her white arms sleek in a sleeveless dress. Familiar handwriting was scrawled on the picture's back: *Wahrstett, 10 Februar 1947.* I turned on the bedside lamp, held the photo to it and looked at the welt on her neck. *A dog scratched me when I came to Canada*—that was how my mother explained her daily scarves, worn to cover most of her throat. But she came here in 1950.

A car wheeled into the driveway. I went to the front door

and raised the window blind. I watched my mother pull the garage door open with one hand. She parked the car inside.

Dressed in a yellow blouse and white pants, her blue scarf caught in her own breeze, my mother frowned at the ragged grass and lugged bags of groceries up the walk. I opened the door and noted her tight lips and the grey roots of her dyed black hair. When I held out my hands to help her, she looked away and bustled past, the bags grazing my legs. As ever, she was pushing her pain in my face. I blew out a heavy breath, but she didn't react.

"Have you eaten?" she said. "Everything's on the stove. Sit down and I'll heat it up."

She flicked on the kitchen light and the glare stung my eyes. After turning on the stove's front burner, she put some groceries into cupboards and went back to the stove and removed a pan's lid. With her wooden spoon she stirred the food, then stopped and unpacked more bags. I knew the cupboards and cold-room already had enough meat and canned goods to feed two people for months, but maybe that was the point.

Her back turned to me, she tapped salt into the food. "When did you get here?"

"An hour ago, I guess."

"Will you stay in Toronto now? I bet you still don't have a good job."

"You know I've been staying at my friend's place downtown, the place I called you from. I might apply at your factory for the security job. I just need to make money so I can travel again."

"You stupid, they filled up positions in April! I've told you _so_ many times—apply early if you want to work there." The way she drew out the _so_ made me look away, at the kitchen door. At least I didn't want to punch her. I did that when I was sixteen: a shot to the shoulder that crumpled her against a wall. For the next three days she confronted me and rolled up her sleeve, showing me the purple puck-sized bruise.

Now she poured a glass of milk and put it beside me.

"Why don't you go back to university and do your Master's?" she said.

"Maybe one day."

"Just maybe? I give you everything and you do nothing."

She went back to the stove.

Our talk was bowling down the old lane and soon the pins would smash and fall. No-one ever won and the explosion echoed: in the kitchen, then in my head when I left. And I always left.

I tried to stay calm, keep my voice even. "Mom, in the war you were at your mother's the whole time—right?"

For a second she stopped stirring, and the smells seemed to thicken, to coagulate in the kitchen air. I slid the window open. Somewhere near, a man shouted a woman's name.

"Mom, I know the soldiers came into villages—"

The crackle of frying food filled the air, interrupting me. She'd lifted the lid and with her spoon pushed the carrots, mashed potatoes and pork chops onto a plate. Some of it spilled onto the stove. She swore in German, and brought me the steaming meal.

A heap of food filled my plate, right to the edges. I missed meat; my downtown friend was vegetarian. I started to eat. I just wanted to enjoy my mother's cooking, not try to tear some awful truth out of her. But the thought of stopping now bothered me even more.

"Who came to your village—the Russians?"

Her eyes watched my fork as I lifted a speared bit of pork to my mouth.

"We called them Cossacks." She went to the sink and washed the pan. "But that was so long ago, it's not true anymore."

I stared at her scarf, and my mouth was full when she brought me a napkin, folding it as she approached. Her hair swung slightly as she walked, veiling the parts of her neck the scarf had left exposed. I couldn't ask about the scar.

"Where's my package?" I asked. When I phoned her from my friend's place, she'd said that a package had arrived from Europe.

My mother laughed—a happy laugh, a laugh without malice.

I put down my knife.

"What's so funny?"

"Finish your food. I tricked you!"

"And you wonder why I'm never here."

I'd muttered the words, but she had already bustled out of the room. I was left with the last bit of meat and a reminder. She'd always use lies to control me, and I had to accept that: the way she went on.

My mother returned with a marble cake. A thick slice with vanilla ice-cream appeared on a dish beside me, and before I could ask she topped up my glass with milk.

Her voice hit me when, my plate clean, I pushed back my chair and stood.

"Will you stay tonight?"

I didn't answer. Answering was impossible, as was looking in her direction, so I just turned and walked down the hall.

At the front door I paused for a long minute, flicked on the porch light and went outside. The garage door groaned when I opened it. I switched on the inside light and uncovered the lawnmower, unscrewed the gas cap and tilted the tank into the light. Low. I got the plastic gas container, adjusted the nozzle and filled the tank. With a rag I removed grease from the tank's lip, then made sure the spark plug was tightly screwed in. Gently, I turned the mower on its side and with a sharp stick I scraped the dried grass from the hubs and the wheels themselves. I rubbed my finger along the dull circular blade.

Front lawns were shining under porch lights and street lamps. I held the mower's handle, surveyed the houses: all quiet, their windows lit. Pulling the cord would explode the silence and upset the neighbours. I wheeled the mower back into the garage and slowly shut the creaking door. I could sleep in my old room and cut the lawn tomorrow. Spare my mother some shame.

# 5. Flaco Was Here

Just so he could brag at home, that straw-hat boy came thousands of miles to a jungle full of men with guns. That blue-eyed *norteamericano* traded his big house for a concrete box with a rattling iron roof, our wonderful state farm, where tortillas, meat, beer and young women only showed up in dreams. Flaco the Taco was just one more skinny volunteer, an *internationalista*. I'd seen his kind before. On that day in '87 (I think), he swung his machete right beside me, slashing the grass between the coffee bushes and trying to work harder than the rest of us, the ones who belonged there. He'd been with us a week and I never spoke to him, I didn't even smile. I looked away—and looked back. Flaco grinned at cockroaches, vultures, snakes, and even our wrinkled cook, whose coffee and beans weren't exactly helping his diarrhoea. It's funny, though, how every night he jumped out of his sleeping bag and ran from the compound into the grass. The soldiers imitated him, the quack that started the river out of his ass, and the way his butt coughed—like a tree frog or a sick machine-gun. When I patrolled at midnight I heard it all. Even the nighthawks stopped flying, just to listen. Maybe that's what Flaco remembers best about our great Nicaraguan revolution: his nights under a million stars, the wet grass tickling his cheeks and his own revolution churning up his guts. While we laughed at his pale behind, pointed our Russian rifles at it, then went back to the job, holding our guns as we entered the bush and listened for strange noises, for the men who wanted to kill us.

On the day I remember, an engine snorted along the stony road. A jeep stopped at the foot of the hill. Our boss Carlos told us to keep cutting, before he ran down to the road, glad to give his arms and back a rest. The sun sat right on top of us and smothered the air in our lungs, but I didn't care. We'd be quitting soon anyway. Flaco was still swinging his machete and so was everyone else, a dozen baseball caps bobbing up and down, sweat blinding their eyes in that thick June heat.

The guy in the jeep was wearing fatigues and a beret, obviously army and important. He poked his finger into our boss's chest, which I knew Carlos didn't like. Small guys hate big guys to begin with, especially those who act tough. But Carlos knew how you listen to soldiers: smile, nod, say yes to everything. They went away and you did what you wanted. Unless the *contras* were around, in which case you wanted as many soldiers there as possible. The year before Flaco came, the *contras* burned the farm to the ground, all three buildings. That left us, the workers from Matagalpa, with concrete floors scorched black. We had to build the farm again.

The jeep roared away and Carlos watched it disappear around a corner before he slipped off his red bandanna, and slowly retied it. A pretty boy, he loved his shiny black hair. He was also a true believer, one of our free-homeland-or-death types.

He called me down to the road. I was the oldest worker: he trusted me. I didn't talk.

"Did you see that guy's green eyes, Ernesto?" Carlos kept clasping his hands together, like he was shaking hands with himself, like he'd won a drinking game or beauty contest or something.

I shook my head.

"He says there's fighting twenty kilometres away."

"It's been closer."

He nodded at the hillside—everyone sat in the grass, watching us. A monkey screamed in the trees behind me and I wanted to scream back. They never gave you peace. Hell must be full of them.

Carlos lowered his voice: "I'm worried about Flaco. An *internacionalista* gets killed, the newspapers around the world are full of it and pow! We lose 5000 free workers. Especially the blondies in Managua who fuck us for the revolution."

60

"Poor you."

Carlos laughed, and squeezed my arm. "Get the guys, but don't tell them about the fighting."

Later, our machetes balanced on our shoulders, our ears trying to shut out the monkey cries, we walked down the road and everyone asked Carlos about the jeep. The little whore told them what he'd told me, which made me look like a bastard for saying nothing. He always did that just so he could be the hero, the only one who thought us tough enough to handle bad news. To handle fear. He took Flaco aside and called him Walter, his real name. Carlos said that if the fighting came closer, he'd be driven back to the city in the truck. Smart, I thought. Though when we got back to the farm, I saw that the truck was gone. I asked around. It was in the city, a hundred kilometres away, and not expected back until tomorrow.

After lunch, Flaco crawled into the verandah hammock—to read. He couldn't relax and do nothing, he was lost without a book in his hand. That boy. He even carved "Flaco Was Here" in the post beside the hammock. But I saw him shake his head at the workers who shuffled up and asked about his country. He said he had to study Spanish grammar. Why? He spoke okay. He was just a snob.

I stretched out on the verandah bench. There was shade and it was mostly quiet. Everyone else was sleeping off his lunch inside the concrete walls. There was no coolness there, just less heat. Heat blurred everything: the white clouds stuck in the sky, the soldiers moving in twos near the bush, the green hills riding the land right to the blue mountain horizon. The farm was awful. Thank God I needed to sleep all the time, and the others let me. Of course, I only complained in my head—the job was much better than my last one. In Matagalpa. For twenty years I buried old people. Then, for the last ten before I worked on the farm, I put young men and even women into the ground, fifteen- and eighteen- and twenty-year-olds. Dozens of them, and not just strangers.

Luca, my eldest, had fought for the *guardia,* and Roberto joined the *Frente.* Enemy sides, till my boys joined our most popular army: the dead. I pulled bits of shrapnel out of Roberto's back and head, counting the purple holes before I put him in the long wooden box.

"Hey, Ernesto."

Flaco sat beside me, smiling. And I could feel my face smiling back—what was wrong with it? Did my face have its own brain?

"Ernesto?"

The bastard even knew my name.

"What is it, Flaco."

"The guys told me you know the whole village. I met a girl and wonder what you know about her."

Incredible. This fool who ran to the village and back every afternoon, now he was picking up girls. The parents would kill him. But maybe they thought he had money, could get her a better life—

"Ernesto, she works in the shop. Long brown hair, and she wears the same orange dress every day. It goes down to here." Flaco swiped his hand across his knees. "When I give her my cordobas and ask for a Coke, she just smiles. But yesterday I tried to talk to her, and—" His mouth hung open. "And she said nothing. She just put a hand on her hip and kept looking at me, until her mom pulled her away."

"She's deaf and dumb, Flaco. From birth."

His head drooped, and I almost felt sorry for him.

I stood up. I had to get away. Though I was so tired I lay right back down on the bench and closed my eyes. I prayed he'd take the hint. No—he kept making noise in my ear.

I opened my right eye slightly.

He was leaning forward, elbows on his knees.

"Ernesto, you remember life before the revolution—are things better now?"

"My sons are dead."

He squinted at me, and I got up on one elbow.

"Flaco. I will die here. But tomorrow you can take a plane and go to a place with toilet paper to wipe your ass. Don't you see—"

Suddenly he slapped the top of my head, jumped up and started stamping his foot on the concrete.

"*Chinga tu madre!* What are you doing?" I jumped up too, my fist pulled back and ready to punch him.

He moved his foot. I saw the mashed-up scorpion.

"Gentlemen." Carlos approached and looked first at the floor. "The new man, Pepe—he's gone. Disappeared. I need someone to replace him on patrol." Carlos put his hand on Flaco's shoulder. "Will you get up an hour early tomorrow and help us out?"

I guessed that Carlos was desperate, but I didn't know why. Flaco nodded. He was desperate too.

When Ignacio started telling everyone that Flaco saved my life, I couldn't believe it. I told Ignacio that scorpions had already stung me a dozen times, and he shot back, yeah, but now you're old, your blood is not strong enough to fight the poison. Ignacio was a bastard. I understood him, though— like all of us, he was bored, so making a man feel fear was something to do.

That night, blue shadows covered the hills, the mountains were dark and for the first time in months there was no guitar on the verandah. Some guys were taking their second siesta, sleeping off their dinner of beans and sweet coffee, while other guys were sitting around and staring at their feet, the bush, the purple light in the sky. It was supposed to be the best time of the day, when one of the guys would play ranchero songs, the sad songs we all knew. Last night we'd all yelled at Flaco, *Baile! Baile! Baile!* and that skinny white kid had danced for us, hopping from foot to foot and spinning around like a drunken monkey. Maybe it was true what Carlos said—Flaco helped our morale. So why did Carlos want him to patrol?

I found our boss at the end of the verandah, sharpening his machete with a flat rock. He sat on the railing and made long smooth strokes. He smiled at the blade.

"Hey Carlos."

He kept on stroking, and the veins bulged in his arms.

"Carlos, remember what you said about all the bad press if Flaco gets wounded, or captured, or even killed? What about scaring away the foreign volunteers?"

"It might be good for us, Ernesto. The Yankees pay the *contras* to destroy our revolution. So, if the *contras* kill Flaco, a Yankee, the American people will realize they are paying men to kill their own brother. All the secret money Reagan gives the *contras*, it will have to stop. The Yankee president will be exposed as a traitor to his own people—can you imagine? If he's lucky, Flaco won't even die. If he does, he'll be a martyr."

"Flaco's a Canadian, not a Yankee."

"Same thing."

I walked away, disgusted. But I had an idea.

He was sitting on top of a rock behind the compound. Big surprise—he was reading, using the last light in the sky. The river gurgled behind him.

"Hey Flaco, tonight I'm doing the shift before you. I'll come wake you up."

He shut his book and gave me that grin.

"Tell me the truth," I said. "Why are you here?"

"To show support."

"Support?"

I spat at his feet, which was the nicest message my brain was flashing to my mouth.

When I came to get him at 5.30, he was already standing on the verandah, in the morning dark, a rifle slung over his back. He was tall, I allowed him that.

I led him to the hammock and took his gun.

"What's going on?" he said, as I motioned for him to lie down. He did, and I threw a blanket over him, put the rifle

64

in his hands. I told him to just relax, stay awake and listen. Not to move, no matter what. I walked away to do his patrol, which meant an hour of extra work.

I stood between the trees, where it was noisy and black. The cicadas and tree frogs played their little orchestra, just the way I liked it. Also, I liked to be alone. Jungle creatures didn't mind one or two guests, but when ten, twenty, 50 men were cracking the leaves with their boots as they moved through the trees, the animals went into their holes and waited for the shooting. Usually, though, the *contras* just sent a few scouts ahead of their detachment. Scouts weren't shy and their rifles had night-vision scopes. Anyway, they had to find you first, and that was why I hardly moved. Plus that night I just wanted one thing—rest. I leaned against a tree, scratched my ear, looked for stars through the treetops and waited—

"Ernesto."

Impossible! The kid was here.

"I just spoke to Carlos," he said, his elbow hitting mine. "He wants us to go back and forth in a 100-metre arc, straight ahead and just inside the bush."

Flaco was excited, so I pinched his arm. "Had your shit yet?"

That shut him up.

Before we went anywhere I told him to wait, let his eyes adjust to the dark. When he proved to me he could make out the shapes of trees, a bush, a hanging vine, I showed him how to walk quietly. We started. For ten, fifteen minutes we went forward, stepping over fallen trees, loosening the vines that wrapped around our legs. We crossed a ravine and I showed him how to use branches like balancing ropes. He was being quiet, everything was going well. Until my left foot twisted in a hole and I fell hard. Face first. My ankle throbbed, pain jumped up my leg—for sure my ankle was sprained. Maybe broken. When the kid tried to help me I told him to let go or I'd shoot. Slowly, I stood and leaned back against a tree. All

65

the insect noises stopped, which was not good.

"Don't move," I told him. I wanted to cry, my foot hurt so much. Cry, scream, punch the tree, punch Flaco. But I had to stay in control.

"Flaco, tell me something. Whisper. Where else have you gone in our country? What did you like best?"

"Leon, Managua…but mostly Granada. I swam every day and had the whole lake to myself."

"You mother-fucking idiot!" Anger thundered in my brain, but I made a great effort to speak calmly. "Flaco. In that lake are freshwater sharks."

A flapping sound scared us. A hawk went by, leaving the bush. I gestured to Flaco and we went on. My ankle felt a bit better. We took one step at a time, scouting our section. We stopped where the jungle ended, at a field. Yellow, orange and red light made a band across the far mountains. We were safe. No cracking branches, no popping machine-guns, no mortars, no screams like when someone lost a leg. I told Flaco we were going back, then I saw the boot.

I dropped to my knees and reached out.

It was Pepe, the guy who'd disappeared.

I hissed at Flaco: "Go five steps back. No noise. Just stand still and look in a half-circle, left to right, then reverse. Keep your finger on the trigger."

Pepe's body was half-covered by a bush and I couldn't tell if he'd fallen that way or if someone had tried to hide him but gave up. I turned him over and my breath stopped. Dark blood smeared his throat, his chin.

"There's nobody around, Ernesto. Ernesto—"

Flaco's hands flopped down to his sides and he almost dropped his gun.

"Help me, kid."

We dragged the body ten metres back into the jungle, hid it under another bush and messed up the trail our boots had made. Heading back to the farm, I didn't tell Flaco what I thought. I just said that Pepe's wife had been cheating on him and he couldn't go on. Suicide, I said. The way to save face. Flaco nodded. He didn't know how hard it is to cut your own throat.

"Don't say a word to anyone," I told him. "I'll let Carlos know. You just go to the party. Eat some meat."

"There's a party and meat because it's Saturday?"

"I thought you were a good socialist. Today's May 1st—International Workers' Day. The bigwigs are coming up from Matagalpa. They know all about you."

Flaco stopped and said he was going back.

I grabbed his arm. "Don't be crazy."

A breeze brought us laughter: women were scrubbing clothes down at the river.

"Ernesto, the *contras* might find his body and desecrate it."

He turned around and I wrenched his shoulder backwards. He fell into the grass.

"Don't be stupid now," I spat. "In the jungle they'll kill you. After they cut off your cock and stuff it in your mouth."

Flaco lay still. His straw hat had fallen off, and his wide blue eyes knew nothing.

"But Pepe's alone," he said, and started to get up. "You're hurt. I could go fast and be back here with Pepe in twenty minutes."

"You'll go with me for food—that's it," I said, grabbing his hand to pull him up. We walked back to the farm, and I tried not to hobble.

Three men with shaved faces came that morning from the agricultural reform ministry. They brought beer, a cow and a flag. I would've preferred just beer. The men sat at a table on the small grassy hill beside the verandah. Carlos and the green-eyed army commander were with them, eating from their heaped plates, and drinking their bottles of Victory beer. Meanwhile the workers, soldiers, and even Flaco, whose elbow rubbed against mine when he forked food into his mouth—we all sat on our bench, plates in our laps. Beef, tortillas, rice, tomatoes. It was the best meal we'd had in months, although the visitors wouldn't give us beer. And the heat that day: the air was like hot wool rubbing your skin when you moved. I was ready to kill someone for alcohol, and so were the guys beside me. Between mouthfuls, we muttered and stared at the dirt floor. Then one of the ministry guys yelled at Flaco to come up, and our skinny *internationalista* gave us a private wink. I smiled. Maybe, I thought, blue-eyes will liberate some beer. The workers whispered the same idea.

Flaco and the government men sat together, laughing and waving their forks like they were scaring away flies. I knew who the flies were. The army guy just farted and said nothing. I took my plate to the hill and sat on the slope, facing the verandah.

The talk suddenly paused, but Carlos started in a loud voice about how hard a worker Flaco was. A ministry guy blabbed about how much our country appreciated young people like him, the foreign symbols of the solidarity of—that was all I heard because I walked away, back to the verandah. All the men sat on the bench or wall, their empty plates in the dirt and their eyes aimed at something behind me.

He'd come down the hill and was swinging a red pail of clinking bottles. Flaco put it in the dirt and motioned me away from the others who scrambled to help themselves. A guitar started. He pulled me by the arm.

We stood near the jungle and I couldn't believe he was keeping me there. He rubbed the sweat off his forehead.

"What's your theory about Pepe?" he asked.

"What's yours?"

"We should get him."

I sighed. Laughter came from the men drinking beer in the shade, their bones weak but their brains happy—while I stood alone with that white boy, my throat like cracked earth.

"The body's gone," I said, truthfully. I told him that some of the men had already taken Pepe away and buried him.

"But what happened, Ernesto? Did he have something some-one wanted?"

I shrugged. "Well, his wife *is* beautiful...."

"Maybe a *contra* killed Pepe to paralyze us. Make us so afraid—"

I heard a bird cry, a high piercing sound, but when I looked at the trees I just saw leaves moving with the breeze. I nodded at Flaco.

"A good theory," I said, and lied: "Ten of our soldiers have been on patrol since we found the body, and no-one has seen or heard anything suspicious."

We turned to walk through the tall grass back to the ver-andah, and Flaco muttered to himself in Spanish. He stopped and touched my arm again. He couldn't stop.

"Ernesto—was Pepe trying to run away? To maybe even join the *contras*?"

*Not to join them,* I told myself. *To escape the target we call home— our wonderful farm.* I'd never tell Flaco what Carlos did to de-serters, what he told me he did to Pepe as a warning. *A collective warning,* Carlos called it. He was our revolutionary true be-liever, and our jailer.

"Your beer misses you," I told Flaco, smiling at the straw-hat boy. A week later he left. He didn't say where he was going, and I don't think he knew. Well, he was here a few years ago, but he loves newspapers so he must know the war's over, the *contras* disbanded. Flaco won't know I'm back in Matagalpa, that some mornings I leave my wooden shack and visit Pepe's widow. She never remarried, even though she's still young and has beautiful hazel eyes. We sit outside on her bench, she hands me a cup of sweet coffee and we talk about the government, the war, Flaco and everything else. Children in navy-blue uni-forms pass us on the dusty road. The children don't have desks at school so they bring their own from home, balanced on their heads. I tell Pepe's widow that poverty will never leave our country. "Like people with money do," she says. "And the dead."

# 6. The Mountain Clinic

Months after my request, a large white envelope slipped through my mail slot: the police report on my father. They call it the "Occurrence Report." I've been poring over it while student essays glower from the end of my desk. Poring over twenty blotched, often indecipherable pages, all stamped BEST COPY AVAILABLE. Many pages include the phrase "partial access granted," followed by whited-out areas. Some are paragraph-thick, others as short and thin as a name. I read and sometimes look out the window at the Montreal afternoon, the April sun blasting into the street and turning asphalt, parked cars, and snowbanks into glare. The report itself has so many blanked-out areas, it too looks like the snow that won't melt. Police snow. Still, my father disappeared in 1966—30 years ago, when I was seven—and now I have a new mound of facts and secrets to fill the hole his absence left. More facts, more secrets. I'll try to fit them in alongside those I already know, along with memories of persons living and dead, of places like the road-hockey Scarborough where I grew up. However, the facts, secrets, and my own imaginings needn't be a hole-filling jumble. They could be tools: precision tools. To measure, mortice, and sand the sides of my father's life, not so different from the way he made window frames for almost two years in his rented Unionville shop that was such a—stop. I'm getting ahead of myself. There's no rush. Still, that's what I sometimes forget, like my bike-lock key or the one for my steering-wheel club. I forget, or I try to make the wrong key work.

While forming these thoughts, I scratch a spot at the back of my head. Lately, students have said I mumble. And my handwriting has cramped up, gnarled, as if something tight in my mind can only come out as such: a stiff-fingered, pressing-down on the page with a pen that blots. All unexpected, because I'm only 37—my father's age when he disappeared—and, well, I'd always thought this age not very old. Maybe it's time to think again.

A few weeks before my father vanished, his father arrived from Austria. Opa was (and is) a short white-haired man in suspenders who talks with his hands held flat out and palms down, like he's patting the air. This August, I hope to attend his hundredth birthday party. But his long-ago visit: it was just three weeks, and I dimly recall his presence in my father's shop on the one day I went along. That day the shop was monsoon hot: everyone sweated and swore.

"*Wo ist Franz?*" Opa asked. He stood on the concrete floor, his brown eyes blinking at the machines and sawdust and belts of sandpaper. His stubby fingers went to his eyes and tried to rub out the stinging sweat. He kept poking away, and finally let his hands drop.

I translated Opa's question for Derek, a tall overalled black man who held a roll of sandpaper.

"He wants to know where Franz is."

Derek shrugged at Opa, and winked at me.

"Walter, tell grandpa your dad's out looking for orders. That that's his job."

"I can't say boss in German." I felt stupid, and Derek gave me a mock-angry look and drew back his hand. Opa stepped in front of him, and Derek laughed.

"I can say boss man in Creole, French and Spanish," he said, "but German, young one, is beyond my abilities."

Opa didn't understand a word and I couldn't translate, but none of it mattered because Derek returned to his belt sander and pressed a button. A roar engulfed us. Opa touched his nose and pulled his finger away—red. He tilted his head back while I ran to the washroom for toilet paper.

A few minutes later, my father strode through the open shipping door, his tie flapping against his white shirt. He looked strange: walking so fast in a hot machinery jungle, where humans couldn't last ten minutes without wiping their faces on their sleeves.

My father suddenly stopped, and I watched his tie settle against his chest. The belt sander droned on. No-one else had seen him come in. His right hand dangled a black briefcase, and it jiggled a bit while he surveyed his workers bent over machines and his own father staunching blood. Franz didn't move, as if the noise and heat had confused him. I think it was only me who saw him hurl his briefcase against the office wall. The black object bounced off, the sound of impact lost in the shop roar. I averted my eyes and went to my broom leaning against the wall. I swept sawdust. When I looked back, my father and his briefcase were gone.

"You phoned him," snarled Franz, who stood with my mother in the kitchen. Opa was shaving in the upstairs bathroom and I was perched on the steps near the front door—hidden from view. Even with the kitchen door closed, my parents' voices floated right to me.

My father's was like a rake scratching concrete, making sparks.

"You told him to come because you said I need help—why? I can do it alone!"

I heard muffled sounds. I raced up the stairs to my room and, not knowing what to do, looked out the window. My friend Marty was walking with his hockey net balanced on his shoulder, his stick in his hand. No way my parents would let me go outside and play. The upstairs bathroom door creaked, and Opa came right into my room, filling it with the smell of shaving cream. His hands were in front of him again, patting down the air. He murmured things in dialect I didn't understand—and put a finger to his lips. He shooed me toward the hall and down the stairs to the front door. We went outside, and I struggled to keep my eyes off Marty in the crescent.

"*Geh' ma arbeiten,*" urged Opa. Let's go to work.

Soon we were stooped over in the backyard. Until my

72

mother called us in for supper, we picked up the fallen pears and plums, dropped them into bushels and dumped the rotten fruit onto the compost heap. Opa kept on nattering in his German dialect and I nodded back, not getting a word.

Scattered across my desk are a dozen white-bordered photos of Opa's stay, square curled mementoes my mother gave me on my recent visit to her Toronto home.

The photos are almost all of my father, grandfather and me, for it's the grand occasion: three generations of male Schwendes. My mother never poses. She orders the poses, pushing each of us into position. She stands us together on the front steps of the house. The photos are taken with black-and-white film, so we're a clump of dark, grey, and pale stalks, flowers planted by the farmer's daughter turned family gardener.

Father is tallest, so he's put in the back. Opa stands in front of his son, and I'm in front of him. No-one smiles. It's the only possible protest, spontaneously chosen by all prisoners. The paving stones are pockmarked, as if soldiers have already swept through the area in front of our house, a battle already fought and decided.

In one photo, my father's mouth is shut, his horn-rimmed glasses askew and the last buttons of his Hawaiian shirt undone, exposing his white gut. He clasps his hands over his crotch, his watch a black band on his wrist. He squints. He is 37, looks 57. His shoulders sag and his torso leans forward, ready to tip. I stand less than an arm's length away, but he doesn't touch me. In most of the photos, I'm half in shadow, my mouth a dark slit like a horizontal keyhole.

Only one shot is not set on the house steps: we stand in our usual clump position, but we're in front of a gigantic flower clock, shaped like a thick wedge on the ground. Perhaps the background made my father feel reflective, or anxious. Flower time, Austrian time—now behind him, watching his back.

73

My father left us two weeks after his father did. Opa was going home, but no-one knew where Franz went.

Perhaps he was smiling when he walked out of the bedroom after a last glance at my mother stretched out under a linen sheet, and a glance at my shut door. Perhaps reversing out of the driveway at 5.30 AM on that August day was like forwarding himself into the proverbial new start, because he thought it so: a bright world that promised better things, events, feelings. He'd only inhabit places where he wouldn't hear the machine roar of doubt—so he told himself. Perhaps as he sat in his Volkswagen, crossing the crescent toward its mouth, my father addressed his neighbours' cars in his fifteen-year-old language: *I'm changing my life.*

He drove through side streets to a southbound road and headed toward the lake, his sunglasses already in his shirt-pocket case, his first disguise the simplest. In the back seat sat his briefcase, work papers within, plus his wallet ($1.26 inside), a cheque made out to a Newmarket magistrate, a spare set of glasses and car keys, a lunch bag of my mother's sandwiches, and a thermos of tea. He'd park near the race-track. He'd lock the car and keep his door and ignition key. He'd have his canvas shoulder bag, a bathing suit inside. In the back seat, he'd also leave his clothes folded in squares: grey dress pants; checked sports shirt; blue underwear; black socks. On the floor, side by side, his black Oxfords. He'd walk to the lake and swim—supposedly. He'd drown—supposedly. His wife and child would be pitied, surely. They would get help, surely. Everyone would agree—a tragedy. All this was part of my father's plan. And the police would dredge the harbour and find nothing.

He drove south on Warden Avenue and reconsidered everything. The sky was yellow-blue and full of light on his left, in the east. His watch said 5.54 AM. In 24 minutes he'd started his future. His head hurt. He looked through the windshield at the empty two-lane road and realized he'd

74

been scratching his scalp, gouging a spot near the back. He pulled his hand away and tried to believe in hope, not the red mark on his finger.

At an intersection he turned west and began the slow descent to Woodbine Avenue. He drove past squat bungalows, their long verandahs and close-cut lawns. His mind replayed the voices and images of last night, his talk with Leona, my mother: behind the closed bedroom door, she'd rasped at him yet again about money. How he needed to give her more so she could make the monthly mortgage payment; how she didn't call his father to bail him out with a loan; how she never thought he was telling the truth about how many orders he'd secured; how he never explained when he (meaning they) would get paid. Leona also wondered why he'd put 8000 miles on the car in the last six months, and why he'd been to Montreal eleven times and still didn't have a contract with Kaiser Ltd., the big aluminum company he was supposedly soliciting.

Franz hit the brakes too hard and his torso jolted forward, his face almost smashing into the windshield. He stared at the red light and recalled how he'd faced Leona and felt as if everything inside him was a torrent, a rush of blood wanting to burst out of his body with a punch or shove or sprint out the door. He had forced himself to calm down. He'd smiled at her, stretched out his arms and hugged her stiff body. "I'll tell you everything tomorrow," he'd said. Now the red light at Queen and Woodbine turned green, but no-one was behind him. He didn't have to drive.

His mind idled. He felt steady. He could think. He was thinking he needed more time to think. He flicked on his left-turn signal light and proceeded south toward the beach, but instead of parking his car he kept on driving toward the expressway. He headed toward the western end of downtown, where used-car dealerships lined the road and no-one knew him, no friends or suppliers, no clients or writ-serving sheriffs. He drove past the ferris wheels and roller coasters of the

75

Canadian National Exhibition—the "Ex." He nodded at that. Things were starting to fit together. To feel squared off. Everything that happened was meant to be. Yes. He slipped his index finger under his glasses and rubbed his right eye. Yes. He could believe anything. And when a Boeing 727 roared overhead, out over the lake, he watched it become a speck and vanish. He thought that was a good sign. No—the best.

The family car was found by police, parked on a side street by Woodbine Racetrack. That is a fact, verified by the Occurrence Report and a *Toronto Star* article I also have. Where my father went after he dumped our Volkswagen, I can only imagine. Though the article does note that, soon after Franz's disappearance, provincial police found a car registered in his name, a car wrecked near Kingston. So he left us and drove east. Like me, he probably chose to do things the hard way, so he likely drove for half the night. In my mind's eye I see it: somewhere past Gananoque, where the highway runs down along the river, the weather turns foul. His car spins out in a storm and hits a tree. He walks away from the crash. As I have done, he hitch-hikes.

"Sir," says the boy, "you're pretty wet." Despite the pounding rain, the boy presses on the gas and his pickup wheels spit gravel, fishtail back onto the river road, his wipers like frenzied arms waving at him to stop.

"Wet is not so bad," says Franz.

"Is that your car crashed against the tree back there?"

"I didn't see it. I just left my friend's house and need to catch a bus in Kingston."

"With no umbrella—right."

"I must reach Kingston."

"Relax. We'll be there soon, unless this storm wants my car to smash like that other one, in which case we'd be crippled and you'd miss your bus and I'd lose my job, and I wouldn't be able to afford tuition so I'd become a semi-paralytic greasy-spoon cashier, for *life*. Which would be fate's big knee to my small groin. Anyway, I'm Darren. You?"

"Herbert."

My father looks over the bearded kid in his T-shirt and faded jeans. Franz points at the speedometer.

"Slow down for the curves, unless the rain lets up."

Darren glances again at the man's face—at the raindrops on his glasses—and eases up on the accelerator.

The slam of rain weakens, merely spots the windshield.

"Psychic," smiles Darren, and my father frowns.

"Psycho?"

The boy shakes his head. "Knowing what'll happen, versus crazy."

Franz sees a blue sign for Mallorytown Landing.

"I don't know," he mutters.

Kingston is brick and limestone and few cars. The rain has stopped and mist hangs over an empty lot. At the diner where he works, Darren arranges a free breakfast for Franz. After inhaling a plate of bacon and eggs in about three minutes, he orders another and asks the waitress not to tell his benefactor, slips her two dollars though the special was a buck and her mouth gapes and she sputters thank-you. He eats his second meal while watching the sun struggle through the mist. He has to find the bus station, but first he must do something else.

The washroom door locked behind him, he runs hot water over his hands and vigorously soaps his left, then attempts to slip the gold wedding band off his finger. It moves, but he can't get it past the knuckle. He sluices more water, water so hot it burns him, and he soaps even harder, turning the ring around before he tries again to push it off. It bites the skin. He grinds his teeth, shoves it again. It scrapes the knuckle and goes over. He puts the ring in his pocket, trying not to think about the inscription.

"Going, Herbert?" Darren calls out. He's aproned and

hair-netted behind the counter. Franz adjusts the bag strap on his shoulder, smiles and shakes the young man's hand.

"Thanks again for the lift."

"Whereya off to?"

"Vancouver." Franz puts his sunglasses on. Three hours later he's asleep on the Greyhound bus to Montreal, his head cushioned by his jacket against the window, a spine-cracked novel in his lap. He has already read the first chapter, but it bored him. Novels are too slow. He can't flip pages forever, waiting to learn what happens next to someone else.

Hours later, he stands in the foyer of a Pointe-Claire apartment building. Darkness has shut down the Montreal suburb. After the car crash and bus-ride, his bones are like empty hangers in a closet, his flesh heaped on the floor, his blood gone. My father presses a tenant-panel button, and pushes his glasses up against his forehead. He wonders whether everything he's done is wrong. Perhaps he should return to the bus station, to Toronto, to the car he parked near the racetrack. He shakes his head. That was 30 hours ago. Still, he thinks he could go home and tell Leona he suffered temporary amnesia—or no, he could be honest. He could say what he hated, what made him scream at the windshield when he drove home from work every day for the last month.

"Hello—who is it?" The woman's voice crackles out of the intercom slits, and Franz stands mute.

"Is there a problem?" The voice now sharp, impatient.

"It's me."

"Frank? What is—?"

The buzzer goes off and he thinks again of running away, but instead he opens the door, steps into the elevator and tries to decide how much he'll tell Anick and whether she'll believe any of it. The elevator creaks upward and he wishes it would go on and he could stay alone in the wood-panelled box until he reaches someplace quiet and empty. Franz pinches his arm. He is doing what he often did as a child: daydreaming a reality opposite to his own. The elevator stops. The door shudders open. He puts one foot forward, then the other.

Anick: he wonders how she'll look. Made-up, scented, smiling? Shoulders slumped, glasses on, ashes stuck to her shirt? Angry at the intrusion after a workday and on the eve of another?

Her door swings open. A green towel is wrapped around her body, her blond hair curled forward like dual crescent moons. Her right hand covers her face.

"Don't touch me," she mumbles through fingers, "or you'll get sick too."

She drops her hand. Cold sores mark the skin near her mouth.

"I'm already sick," Franz tells her, and when he opens his arms he closes his eyes and keeps them closed as he feels her body, its pressure. He holds her, and decides what he has to learn: to stop wanting. To accept. Or if need be, if nothing is offered, to accept that. An anchoring thought, one he hopes will let him float in the same place for an hour, until he sinks into dreams, into the sea bed he knows, the one where dark shapes float past. Always past.

Rain has turned the snow into muddied grey veins of slush. It's an early April Saturday, the school term ends in a month, and all I can think of is the Occurrence Report and my August trip to Austria for Opa's party. Yesterday I was totally unprepared for my morning class—not a serious problem, since a half-dozen years of teaching have taught me how to fake it. Still, my class was troubling.

I stood before rows of slouched and upright students, all of them waiting for me to lecture about what I supposedly knew. I looked around. Some kids looked as bleary as I surely did, their heads lolled back and eyes half-closed. A few keeners notwithstanding, no-one wanted to be here at 8.33

AM. Or ever. Drizzle dripped down the windows. Nothing was on the blackboard except my daily quotation.

"Walter," said a front-row girl, her product-heavy hair curlicuing around her face and onto her shoulders. "You're already covered in chalk."

Some students laughed. She was right: the sleeves and lapels of my blue jacket were spotted with white dust. I still couldn't last a class—or, apparently, start one—without blotching my clothes and face and hair with chalk.

"Good quote," called out a buff guy in the back. I'd scrawled a bit of Martin Amis on the board: "Addictions can't be all bad. At least they get you out of bed."

"I can't read the first word," said another guy in the back, and the girl beside him said "*Addic*tions" in a loud voice. More people laughed.

I nodded at the boy and saw 30 pairs of eyes watching me. I turned around, wiped off the Amis quotation and wrote *Bruno Schulz*.

I faced the class. Three gulls sailed by the windows, and three students yawned.

"Okay," I said, and put on my best impassive face. "Let's play the honesty game. How many of you *haven't* read the Schulz story?"

Two-thirds of the students raised and dropped their hands.

"Does the guy really turn into a crab?" asked a boy who hadn't spoken all term.

"But—" added a front-row girl "—how can he become a *crab*, be boiled to death by his wife, then come back to life and scuttle away? Like, are we supposed to *believe* that?"

Some students groaned.

"Thanks a *lot*," drawled another girl.

"Well, we're sup*posed* to have it read for today," said the first girl. "It's four pages!"

"I started but didn't finish," shrugged a back-row guy.

Some students looked at their feet; some at other students; some at the windows.

"Okay," I said, my voice brisk, controlled. "Let's do something different. Take out some loose-leaf."

Paper was pulled out of binders and notebooks, sometimes passed from hand to hand.

"Schulz's story is about his father," I said, my voice calm. All eyes locked on mine. "I mean—his father fictionalized. We all have fathers. Somewhere. Maybe even in our homes."

A few people snickered. Students love irony, but they always call it sarcasm.

"So here's what you'll do. Don't think. Just jot down everything in your head right now about your father. Don't sign the page if you don't want to. This is just brainstorming. All our coursepack stories have central father characters, so you'll have to get into father-thinking mode for the final essay, no matter what topic you choose."

Within seconds, some students had bent their heads and were writing rapidly. Others gazed at the board. A few stared at me, and one girl's mouth was open. I placed an empty desk near the door.

"Sorry to interrupt," I added, my voice lower. "Take as long as you like. But remember—it's not for marks. And don't worry about your handwriting. Put your paper on this desk when you finish and then you can leave. Make sure you've read the Schulz story for Monday."

Every writing hand moved across a page. I sat at my desk and observed the hunkered bodies, everyone thinking about his or her father, everyone too tired to obscure the thoughts and feelings that churned in their respective minds. I thought about my grandfather. He'd just sent me a carefully penned letter and crowed about how, though he was only the *second* oldest person in his province, the oldest just lay in bed. How, for the last decade, this 102-year-old woman hadn't been seen in church, whereas he went for daily walks and, every Sunday, attended the 7 AM mass—the earliest. He'd ended that last sentence with an exclamation mark.

Students passed in the halls, their footsteps getting louder before they faded. In front of me, a boy stood up and slung on his daypack, put his sheet on the desk and left. A girl did the same. Then another.

The class emptied in twenty minutes.

I brought the pages to my desk and glanced through them, pulling out the ones with the fewest words. One page had a point-form list, printed in pencil, without a name at the top.

> my dad
> will the radiation work
> will he die
> will he live
> whats going to happen
> when will I see him again
> I miss him
> why does this happen to him

The page looked up at me, like it was lying on its back. I knew the handwriting. The girl who wrote it was eighteen, but the script was like a child's. I spread my fingers over the page and crumpled it, closed my eyes and squeezed the page into a ball. I held it for a while, knowing that for Monday's class, I'd have to flatten and smooth out the page, perhaps leave it under some books. As if that would change a thing.

The Occurrence Report has sat on my desk for two days. At night, it's reflected in my window and becomes its double. I read and reread the report. Sometimes I start at the end or in the middle, and read toward the first page. Odd how my tool-and-die-maker father, the Austrian immigrant who left his family, has become royalty: in the report, he possesses a multitude of titles. The missing person. The reported missing person. The victim. The subject. Schwende. The missing subject. The missing man. All of these titles remind me of something I've thought before: my father could be anyone. I mean: does who he is even *matter*? Any tall man

82

would do. With some grey hair, glasses and hands callused by work. Yes, and a certain kind of cragged, ruddy face, the breathing light.

On a strangely cold Montreal day last summer, when people went around in long sleeves and pants, I saw the man who could be him.

It happened near the Jacques Cartier monument at the base of Mont-Royal Park. Cartier, his frock coat open and right hand raised, his fingers stretched toward the city. Just past the statue is the bench where I sat after hours of meandering, a bench at the start of the gravel path that disappears in the trees. Exhausted, I saw an old man come and sit down beside me. I fell asleep.

I didn't dream, and he was there when I woke. Smoking a cigarette, he gazed across Park Avenue. Red and white jerseys swarmed up and down a soccer field. The man's elbows were propped on his knees; his rolled-up shirtsleeves revealed arms almost completely hairless. Like mine, I thought, and leaned forward so I could see him better. His face was grey-stubbled and sun-browned; purple veins showed in his neck; his fingers were thick and slightly bent, as if used to lifting heavy objects. The plastic bag at his feet spilled fronds of carrots and scallions.

I pulled my face away. Sure. It could've been him. That man sitting beside me, smoking and watching soccer—sure, he could've been my father. He could've turned to me and told me what he'd done, where he'd been, why he'd left us. He could've explained that he was simply unable to get enough orders for his business, that his potential clients were racist, that they didn't like his German accent. Sure. He could've told me that he left the sagging, downturned mouths of his fellow Austrian villagers for a better life, and guess what? Austria, he could've scoffed, and leaned forward, touching my knees with his—look at a world map and you'll see Austria, a small red shit in the middle of Europe. Now look at Canada and you'll see an even bigger shit—and still red. Yes. Plus this man on the bench could've told me something else, something about a faraway part of the country, but I knew about that because I'd been there. He could've told me that the work-sites up north and out west were full of men like him, men gone grey and bald and gutted, men busted up by faith in the big-house dream, men who still hoped that time and endless bush would heal them.

Yes, the man hunched on the bench could've been my father, could've withdrawn a handkerchief and daubed away my doubts and his guilt. But he wasn't. And when he gave me a slight nod and picked up his bag of vegetables and strolled away, faster than I'd imagined he could walk, I thought to myself: it doesn't matter at all.

My father: I keep killing him, then I bring him back to life. Like the air in my lungs, it's as if he always leaves but never leaves.

Dirty dishes, immaculate books—my apartment lies on a street near the Montreal harbour. Boats sometimes bellow, train-horns blast from the nearby sidings. I'm being called by someone, being told something. I need time: time could pry open the window, let secrets gust into the room and settle. Time helped by thought. So: let the mind shovel. Let it dig the ditch and find the stones. Some are here, in Montreal.

It's September '66, a late afternoon in this city. In my mind's eye, I see him.

The bright lights and colours, the women and their glances, the glass reflections, the wafts of competing perfumes, the mix of spoken French and English and Greek and Italian—Franz lets it all wash over him. He strides on the gleaming tiles of Eaton's, passes the polished chrome edges of counter displays. He stops before a profusion of boxes and jars and tubes: the azures, carmines, cherrys, limes, pinks and turquoises. The cosmetic splendour. Anick stands ten steps away, and her blond hair swings when she leans over the counter and listens.

"*Quelque chose de gratuite aujourd'hui?*"

He sees her hand a small silver box to a dark-haired, short-skirted woman. In his peripheral vision, colourful bodies swirl past. The cacophonous clack of heels. He thinks of saw blades, brown sandpaper, roaring machines. Franz rubs his eyes, rubs away the beginnings of tears. He scratches his head, and must will his hand back down to his side. Shoulders slumped, he stands still amid the colours and brightness and well-dressed people, promising himself that if he *does* fail, if his attempt at reinvention collapses into penury and despair, he'll return to the bridge outside his village and do what other failed locals do: throw himself into the shallow river.

Franz forces himself to stand straight, to align his silver tiepin perpendicular to his gold tie. He pushes the knot up and tight, fluffs the folded handkerchief in his breast pocket, slips both hands into the pockets of his new black suit. He moves toward Anick's back.

She knows his step, turns before he can surprise her.

"Frank!"

She hugs him, her weight sagging against his. He takes it, luxuriates in it. Franz loves the way this fragrant muscled body melds into his, her arms cinched around his back and her cheek pressed into his chest. He doesn't move. He just stands in his suit in the cosmetics department, Anick's arms around him.

When she takes his hand, his fingers feel her rings—one of which he bought her—and his wrist touches her bracelets, her watch. Anick grabs her handbag from behind the counter, waves to her co-worker and leads him down an aisle to the revolving oak-and-glass doors. He pushes himself into one space with her and they're nudged into a cool fall afternoon. About a month after he left us. Does he think about that? Yes, and tries to replace the thought with another: of his hand and how it swings in Anick's as they stroll up Peel toward Mont-Royal Park. Franz does forget what he left behind, what he's done, for right now he's conscious only of fingers laced in his and the sight before him: the steep road; the crimson, orange and yellow leaves of maples; the gravel path that curves to an observation-deck high above the city. As a breeze blows over him, my father thinks again of how much he likes to look up and ahead, to feel his shoes moving on even ground.

He and Anick saunter along the path through the trees, and a policeman on horseback trots past, headed toward the base of the park.

"Will you get another car?" asks Anick, who grins at the couple who pass them. The jean-jacketed man and woman wrinkle their noses and laugh at a pile of horse manure.

Franz squeezes Anick's hand. "Will you buy the car?"

"Will you live with me for more than three days in a row?"

He squeezes her hand again, quickly, but with less pressure. He stops walking. Below them, the grassy hillside is full of people reading or otherwise enjoying the day. Couples lie together. Parents and children toss balls back and forth; some children roll themselves down the hill toward the man-made lake. Franz stares, wondering if their shouts will leave his head.

"I often come here with a book," Anick says, and puts her head against his shoulder. "Shall we sit?"

Franz speaks with difficulty, but tries to sound calm.

"Reading...it's so slow! Manuals, guides, maps—yes. But books...not for me. Why spend hours learning how someone lives, when I could use that time to live myself?"

She pulls him away from the hill and they amble again on the path, toward the lookout. In the large stone pavilion behind it, she buys hot chocolate for her and Franz, sits with him on the steps and admires the people who simply mill about, or lean over the parapet and gaze upon the downtown streets. She hasn't said a word since his outburst. She waits.

A gull swerves past, over their heads and out of sight.

Three flags droop on grey poles—Montreal, Quebec and Canada—and Franz thinks they look like cheap curtains, mere folds of red, white, and blue nylon, with a flash of green.

A cyclist weaves through the observation-deck crowd, her red hair flying behind her. Anick sees the woman lose her balance, crash into a couple and fall.

"Look!" Anick grabs Franz's arm.

"Don't worry—she was riding too slow to hurt anyone."

People help the woman to her feet. She's slapping her thighs, appears to be laughing. A body remains on the ground.

Anick stands up. "I'll see if I can help."

"I'll make sure no-one drinks your drink," says Franz.

"You're good," she smiles, and strides off.

After learning that the fallen man has just been stunned, she returns to the steps. Franz is gone. She checks inside the pavilion: people with coffees and books and newspapers. An hour later, when she arrives home, his clothes aren't there and the spare key she gave him lies on her kitchen table. No note. Anick picks up the key and holds it until it's warm in her hand.


It's midnight, and questions appear in my study. They buzz, hit the window, circle, float, and land again. I swat them but they buzz anew. Watching me. Finally the questions must rest. They are old. What is true? Does it matter?

The couple below me are talking in bed. I imagine them touching each other; I touch the blurred, creased report pages. Whatever their words mean, it's something. For the report does report, more precisely record, on pages numbered 000001 to 000020, numerous events of which I was unaware. For example, on 18 August, 1966, my mother phoned police at 11.50 PM—more than 42 hours after Franz left home. Why did she wait?

Dragging operations, carried out by the harbour police, began on 21 August and lasted until the 24th—"with negative results." The report reveals that a doctor, a Salvation Army worker, a Welfare Department employee and a Catholic Settlement House caseworker were all assigned to check on my mother. The four agents of state care. I can hear the hooves. Also: three months after Franz's disappearance, she went to the police station herself. I see it.

She pushes open the glass door of the Metropolitan Toronto Police Station, 41st Division. She pushes slowly, as if afraid the other side will tell her hurtful things. She stands on the lobby tiles, her hat and coat freckled with the first winter snow. Her coat is plain wool and covers a beige skirt and matching jacket. The desk clerk notices her, smoothes down his hair and curses his oily fingers. She moves toward him, her dark hair fringing blue eyes and a face that has the wounded look common to people who arrive at his desk— though, he must admit, she is prettier than most.

"Hello," she smiles. "I'm Leona Schwende, the wife of Franz. Could I please speak with Detective James?" She examines something in her hand. "He's in the homicide division."

"Detective James isn't in, Mrs. Schwende. But I'll see whether I can get Sergeant Lewis."

She is standing motionless when the clerk returns beside a tall bald man with flitting brown eyes. Lewis escorts her down a hall and into a small bright office, its table home to piles of paper, carbons, letters torn open, and a framed upright photograph of a woman wearing pearls. My mother stares and touches her own necklace, imitation pearls she bought on sale at The Bay.

"How are you *do*ing, Mrs. Schwende?" asks the sergeant, who immediately swears under his breath. It's the stupidest thing he has said that day. The woman has recently lost her husband and she has a son to care for—how *could* she be doing?

My mother lowers her eyes. Her shoulders heave, and the sergeant swears again, silently.

She lifts her head. "Sir—"

He is surprised to see her face dry.

"—I'd like to ask a favour."

Lewis studies her. It's a strange case, and for the last three months, he and the other detectives have been having official and water-cooler talks about it. Facts first: Schwende owed $60,000 to various suppliers and had already been served several writs. Also, he had attempted to defraud the government out of unpaid unemployment-insurance remittances. Now the theories: one is that Schwende faked a drowning so his wife would get the $50,000 in life insurance, which they would share at some later date. Another theory is that he crossed the border into the States. Another is that he had a woman hidden somewhere. Still another is that he was killed by the Mafia.

My mother eases out of her coat, leans forward, and Lewis forces his eyes up.

"Yes, Mrs. Schwende?"

"Franz loves hockey more than anything. We watched it on television *all* the time. We listened to it on the radio, too. Please, you have his photograph—give it with a physical description to the television and radio stations. All of them. Especially Foster Hewitt's radio broadcasts."

Lewis tilts his head.

"Smart idea, Mrs. Schwende."

"And Sergeant Lewis—" My mother pauses. When she sees the man's raised eyebrows, she points at the framed photograph on his desk.

"Her pearls are beautiful—are they fake?"

The detective's eyes widen.

"I bought them at Birks."

My mother nods. "You should get them appraised. I don't

mean to be rude. But I was trained as a jeweller in Innsbruck. Unless you know what you're looking at, it's hard to tell what's real."

The Occurrence Report notes the effect of my mother's request, fulfilled at two radio and two television stations. "NEGATIVE RESULTS AT THIS TIME."

It's way past midnight and I rub my eyes—will a genie spring forth? The report's words shift, blur, become tiny crows immured in snow. But outside my window, the snow has melted. I should go to bed.

The last page is dated 20 November, 1976, and titled "Information from Alan Kelman Sheriff Dept." The page explains how, since 1966, Kelman has kept his own personal file on my father, and prior to the disappearance made many visits to Franz's shop and served writs for the Sherriff's Department. The page also details Kelman's recent sighting of my father: on Thursday, 16 November, at 4.45 PM, at Toronto's Eglinton Subway Station, Franz was boarding the northbound Yonge Street bus at platform No. 2 when Kelman spotted him. The sheriff tried to breach a wall of people, but my father saw him and hurried onto the bus. Kelman noted that my father had a moustache and still wore glasses, looked heavier and had less hair.

I can feel it: nerve-jangling, adrenalin-surge panic. Franz would've shoved himself past people and prayed that Kelman wouldn't board the bus and grab his wrists and snap on hand-cuffs, flash a badge at passengers so all could see who was lawful and who not before Kelman tugged Franz down a crowded aisle, off the bus and into captivity.

I see things in the report, and see other things outside it. Some are easily imagined, because I've done them.

After he leaves Anick in the fall of '66, my father uses part of what he calls his getaway money to buy a used Ford pickup.

For a week he overnights in motels and cruises down his favourite Ontario roads, his eyes on the land and his mind on a plan. He drives with the radio on. He drives until he is lost. He takes turn after turn, trusts his sense of direction to get him back to a recognizable crossing, farm, tree, intersection. His preferred landscape is brown fields and green hills. It reminds him of the land outside his village. He drives on Highways 2 and 7, and, between them, the concession roads he discovered on his trips to and from Montreal. He loves those two-lane roads, how they curve, dip, rise, and straightaway past dirt driveways, slatted barns, fronding willows, and lakes that go blue and grey in concert with the sky. He scours the sky for birds—all good omens. Actual signs also attract him, especially of town names. He could read them in a second, think about them for hours. Newbliss, Brighton, Forthton: in earlier times, those names gave him hope.

After that week, my father travels west and north—for work, for decades. Between jobs, he swings back to Scarborough. However, on that day in '76, Kelman's presence at the subway spooks Franz into leaving the city for good.

Far away from people who know him, who want him for various reasons, Franz will get many jobs: tool-and-die maker in a Thunder Bay factory; works-department snow-removal and parks maintenance in Winnipeg; general labourer at the Eldorado Mine in northern Saskatchewan and finally at the Giant Mine outside Yellowknife. He still takes road trips, still needs getaways. One September afternoon he starts a week-long debushing by driving to Edmonton, a styrofoam cup of coffee nestled between his legs. He drives south on the Mackenzie Highway through miles of muskeg that spread to the horizon on both sides. No hills. No elevation. Instead he sees dwarf pines, rock, shrubs, and bushes, all in various combinations of brown and green, as if the earth was in uniform and ready to battle the blue-clad sky. He thinks of rain, thunder, lightning. The sky would win. It had options. It could change.

I sit on a long black couch in the Zurich airport lounge, all glaring lights and moving shapes, my body and brain inert after a transatlantic flight. It's the day of Opa's centenary. My legs sprawled on the grey tiles, I glance at the TV bracketed against a wall. A German news program is on; the male announcer's voice is ridiculously upbeat; I hear exclamations marks after every sentence. 7.16 AM. My Uncle Herbert—my father's best childhood friend—is coming to pick me up and spirit me to Opa's birthday party. I slump lower on the couch, my pack touching my thigh, and I consider a trip to the nearby kiosk for coffee. My pack is dark blue and beat-up: black thread zigzags alongside the zipper at the top, and a few tears mar the front. Scrunched inside are my party clothes: army-rolled dress pants, dress shirt and tie. I hear steps.

Suits and skirts stream past, all the bodies slim, all suitcases held or pulled by long tanned arms. Everyone looks like a perfect example of what they are: purposeful travellers. My father also journeyed here, in Europe, but that was wartime travel: capture travel: flight-home travel. I've heard stories. For once, people—my mother, my Toronto aunt and uncle—wanted to talk. They were there. They saw. They could and can recall, imagine. So I don't have to imagine my father in war. I've heard about the endless grey mud; I've turned away from the acrid, nostril-flaring stink of his clothes. Still, I wonder whether a boy, forced to vanish from his family, must become a man who needs to vanish. Instead of never wanting to leave home again.

My father was in the German army, but not for long. He never did anything for long.

In March '45, in an Austrian village below the Bregenz hills and near the Swiss Alps, the mayor's men shoved Franz and two friends into a truck already jammed with other boys whose heads were lost in outsized helmets, their uniforms flapping like flags. Also in the truck were grey-haired, dead-eyed grandfathers. It was Hitler's desperate, end-of-the-war *Volksturm*. The truck started up and rumbled round the edge of Lake Constance, past the forest slopes veiled with white cherry blossoms, as if the woods themselves wore a winding-sheet that waited prettily for the dead.

Weeks later, outside a German village, the geese lowered their long necks and hissed. My father's squad clumped past, down the mud track into the forest, and minutes later men emerged from behind the thick oaks and surrounded the tramping soldiers. American-accented German commands were yelled, and all Franz understood was *drop the gun*. He looked at his captors and was so shocked he stepped back-wards and tripped over the foot of the boy behind him. Franz was on the ground when a black hand grabbed his tunic and lifted him to his feet, as if he were a pencil.

"*Alles okay?*" asked the officer. Franz gaped. He'd never seen a black man. The prisoners were marched to a barn and told to line up, hands clamped on their helmets. Franz heard his comrade Austrian and German soldiers sniffle, sob, whisper "*Mutti.*" His nose crinkled. He smelt shit. The boy beside him had soiled himself. It was the end. Fourteen American soldiers had guns aimed at the chests of fourteen prisoners. The order came: the prisoners must remove their helmets—but *langsam*, slowly. Very slowly. The Americans gasped, turned to each other and spoke. Lowered their guns. Most of the prisoners were pink-cheeked boys, their hair matted and eyes sunken. The youngest was twelve. An hour later the same black officer stood beside Franz at a crackling fire. Both men watched the ashes spiral into the dark, and the officer offered a cigarette.

"In our country—" he said in German "—we're like you. Prisoners."

Franz sucked on his cigarette and coughed hard. The officer slapped his back, gave him a piece of chocolate and walked away. The prisoners were bivouacked in the barn.

Next morning, they were given mess kits and told to go home. Franz went alone.

His days were full of nights. He often walked in the dark, a thousand kilometres of walking, walking, walking, through fog and mist and rain. Down mud tracks in forests, wet grass, sodden fields; down cratered mud roads. He crossed churning rivers whose rocks gouged his bare feet while he staggered on, holding his boots above his head. They still got wet. In his slow progress south and west toward his village, the rain fell daily, relentless. It made him jealous: a force with a simple destination.

He was always damp and shivering, his skin puckered. He stank. One day, delirious from lack of sleep, he stood in tall grass and swivelled his head, gazed at fields, houses, churches, trees, roads and kerchiefed women who wiped windows and swept doorsteps. Everyone, everything was grey and brown. And all he heard was barking. Dogs were everywhere: behind fences and doors, in barns and houses. A black dog sprang at him from a ditch and Franz faced the dog full-on, pretended his hand held rocks and mock-flung them. The dog growled, but didn't move. Trembling, Franz walked backwards down the road. A loud rumble filled the air and a train passed, compartment after compartment. All the windows were gone, shattered, a row of black holes in their place. He came to a train station. A few men and women lay on the platform, either asleep or scratching themselves. A girl stood among them and smiled. She looked about twelve, her dark hair pinned on top of her head, her dress brown. He lifted his hand in a wave and the girl was hurried away by an older woman, who nonetheless motioned Franz forward and produced a bowl of hot bean soup.

Homecoming: it was just a few days after VE Day. A band played music when he stumbled down the last twisting road and tried to walk with a straight back into his village. Everyone hugged him, and he was pulled into a *gasthaus* where glasses of beer and schnapps were lined up, the room crowded with his family, neighbours, friends. He was fed steaming goulash and dumplings, cucumber salad sprinkled with paprika. Everyone watched him eat and, when he finished, a dirndled woman would refill his plate and people would watch him eat again. Later, he stumbled out of the washroom and a blond barmaid pushed him right back in and kissed him. She pulled down the top of her blouse and directed his face, then she fumbled at his belt. Fourteen years old, Franz wondered if, for such pleasures, other men had to sneak past three armies for three weeks.

A touch on my shoulder startles me.

Before me stands the slightly paunchy Herbert, his face mapped by burst capillaries, his eyes sky blue. He wears a maroon shirt.

"*Gruss Gott, mein Herr*," he says. I stand and we hug.

I shoulder my pack, wondering how he recognized me. I didn't think I looked like Franz, the way my father did in his thirties.

"Straight to Opa's?" I ask, and Herbert doesn't answer. We walk down the hallway. He smiles at me, but we move in silence to the parking-lot. It's quiet, though nearby is the runway and planes landing and taking off. Perhaps the quiet is a result of mountains: grey, jagged, and bright, despite the dishwater sky. In Herbert's dark green Renault, I try again.

"How long to the village?"

He slips a cigarette into his mouth and lights it. He starts up the car and navigates his way onto the highway. Green hills, orchards, church steeples, flowery meadows, dappled cows—the postcard panoramas past. But we're entering it, the picture you expected to see. I know there's more, but don't know what the more is.

"An hour," says Herbert, eyeing the mountains. "But we're not going there."

"Why not?"

He puffs a cloud of smoke into the car.

"Tell me about teaching, Walter." His grin makes his cheeks bulge. "Tell me a teaching story."

"Why?"

Herbert reaches across my knees and pulls a corked bottle from the glovebox. He rolls the bottle off his fingers into my lap.

"Drink. Tell me about your students. You're not married. Is it because you have so many children?"

More postcards appear beyond the window. I uncork the unlabelled bottle and swallow something that makes me cough. It leaves a peach taste in my mouth. While I wipe my nose, Herbert takes the bottle, laughs and swigs.

I pick up the folded newspaper at my feet. *Vorarlberger Beobachter.* 21 August, 1996. Four days after the thirtieth anniversary of my father's disappearance.

"Bad news?" Herbert asks, and prods me again with the bottle.

I drink, but slowly.

"Uncle Herbert—I'll tell you a teaching story another time."

I can't stay awake after Herbert crosses the Austrian border. He drives on highways and narrow roads, through mountains and valleys. The curves tug my body left and right. I only open my eyes on occasion, once in a dark tunnel, then I lapse back into a dreamless sleep until my body is jostled awake by the car lurching over stones. We're driving down a lane of birch trees. Ahead of us sits a wide, white, three-storeyed building with small windows glinting the sun back at the sun. Beyond the building are slate mountains. I glimpse a green wedge of valley, far below me.

"I'll be back in three hours," announces Herbert, wheeling into the parking-lot. He shuts off the car. "That's all they permit you."

"What are we doing here? Where are we?"

He lets his arm hang out his window.

"Herbert, is Opa here? It's a nursing home?"

"Close."

He lights another cigarette, turns toward me. His eyes wet.

"Your father," he says. "A mental hospital. A clinic."

I sit still, jet-lagged, utterly empty of will and feeling.

"What?" I whisper.

Herbert blows smoke out the window.

"How long has he been here?" I ask.

"A few years. I'm friends with a doctor—I got Franz in."

"Who pays?"

"Who do you think?"

Herbert steps out of the car and slams his door. I do the same.

"You?" I say.

He scratches the side of his face, as if he's getting rid of an itch. Cowbells tinkle somewhere, and I'm back in the postcard.

I try again. "Opa pays?"

My arms are shaking. I want to grab this smirking man and shout in his face, snap him out of this stupid game.

"Are you telling me that everyone here *knows*? His sister and father? All the villagers? And for 30 years only *my* family hasn't known?"

I hear a shout from somewhere on the clinic grounds, but I keep gawking at Herbert.

"His sister is my dead wife," he states. "Just your mother knows that Franz is here. She pays."

"What?"

He drops his cigarette and his sandal grinds it into the dirt.

"Walter, the receptionist expects you." Herbert steps into his car and talks through the open window.

"I'll see you right here at five, before his supper."

My body is stone. His words storm in my head, and it's as if my mind hydroplanes, spins in circles, and slams into something solid.

The life insurance. My mother must've used that money. *Life insurance.* Now the words make sense.

After watching the car bump down the lane toward a gate and booth we must've passed, I turn to the wide building and its glinting windows. My head and body feel like a bursting fire. I start to walk and the hot rush leaves, perhaps helped by the breeze. The rush is replaced by a buzzing inside me, like a wasps' nest.

In the foyer, a white-uniformed nurse approaches with a paper bag in hand. She sees me dawdle beside the wooden doors. She is young and lipsticked, her small face framed by a peaked cap that looks like a tiny white mountain. She holds open a door and speaks German.

"Going out?"

"In."

She passes through the doors. Before me stretches a long corridor, and I can vaguely make out a desk. I stand in an open area of beige couches, chairs, and tall potted flowers, all green stalks and red and blue and yellow petals. Fluorescent tubes cast light from the ceiling. Fan blades cut the air. I want to walk, but once more I can't move. My mind whirs like one of my father's shop machines.

Will the sight of him here, today, in this mountain asylum, change anything? Should I just turn and leave? Get the nurse to direct me to a town so I can drink, get away from Herbert and figure out how to reach Opa's party on my own? Herbert would have to deny he took me here, because no-one else knows that my father is alive. Unless they do know and their ignorance is a ruse. But maybe Franz made Herbert promise to keep the secret. My mother might know something—I could ask and, as ever, try to discern whether her words are lies.

Glass cases line each side of the clinic corridor. I step closer. Behind the glass, on levelled shelves, are thousands of items: crafts, paintings, sketches, and other objects. A sign in seven languages tells me what I've already assumed: the artists are the residents. I run my eyes over the shelves. Pen-and-ink grimaces rise from heads half-buried in pillows. A thin clay figure stands with hands on hips. A watercolour of a boat at sea, the blues of sky and boat and water all a different shade. A cat made of seashells. What looks like human hair bandanna-ed around the eyes of a papier-maché head.

"Walter Schwende?"

I turn to face a young man in a short-sleeved pink shirt. He looks like a film student: square black-framed glasses; short blond hair parted in the middle; a thin goatee. He grins, motions, so we walk to his desk and he makes a phone call. After speaking rapid dialect to someone, he tells me in slower, less colloquial German to take the stairs to the second floor and Room 22. As I turn to leave, he says something else.

"You're his second guest this month—that's never happened."

The young man winks at me. His green eyes remind me of my father's.

"Who?" I ask, thinking of Herbert.

"A woman. We can't give out names, though people always want them." He chuckles, shifts a paper on his desk. "Anyway, when someone gives a name we never know if it's the real one. This place is the castle of lies."

"Are you the king?"

He purses his lips and for a second I just look at him, posed behind his wide desk: the seated sphinx.

I climb the stairs to the second floor, and in less than a minute I'm standing in a tiled hallway, outside of an open door. A man watches television. He sits in a wooden chair and listens to a reporter's British accent. The seated man is both staring at the screen and patting the few strands of white hair strewn across his head. His ruddy face is smooth and he wears a creased white dress shirt, cuffed black pants and shiny black leather shoes. It's as if he's dressed for church, for a wedding or funeral. Suddenly his hand stops patting. I

99

look at the TV screen.

Half-hidden in a chest-deep trench, a woman works. She wears a baseball cap backwards and a red bandanna on her forehead. Sweat drips from her chin into the surgical mask that hangs around her neck. With a brush she removes dirt from the eyes and mouth of a boy, black-haired and fully clothed, his body stretched out on a white sheet. Beside her, another woman pushes a long metal rod into the bottom of the trench, withdraws the rod and smells the end. Behind the women, yellow tape flutters around tree trunks, and the camera pans to other women who huddle in a dirt road and hoist a banner: "Women of Srebrenica." One of them pulls a small bottle from her pocket, unscrews the lid and lifts the bottle above her mouth, but the woman beside her grabs the bottle and smashes it on the road. At this moment the man in the chair swings his head around. It's him. His forehead and chin I know from a dozen photos. The grey-green eyes are large behind the horn-rimmed glasses. The eyes laser right through me, into the thoughts behind. I glance away, at the English paperback left on a dresser: *Russia Dies Laughing. Jokes from Soviet Russia.*

"Outside air is better," he blurts in German, and stands up. He moves toward me but stops an arm's length away and stares again. My hands dangle at my sides, my fingers touch air, and everything inside me is moving. I feel like I can lift anything above my head: the dresser, the bed, my father himself.

I want to hold him, but somehow know he wouldn't respond and I'll want to go down the too-bright hall, trying to forget that he doesn't know me.

Just before we pass through his door, a shriek fills the room. A woman's scream. It's from the TV—my father stops, his head up, listening. A purple vein throbs in his neck. He puts a hand on my back and prods me onward.

His speed in the hallway surprises me: the gait isn't much slower than mine. But he doesn't speak until we clear the building and get onto a dirt path that cuts through the crocuses and short grass.

Iron-grey mountains surround us, snow in their crevasses and upper reaches. The sky is pure deep blue, the sun an orange-yellow blaze. More postcard beauty. I keep thinking there are things I should be seeing, but can't.

My father stops, reaches out a hand.

He must want me to note the perimeter fence and its high barbed wire. We're heading right for it. The fence looks like the one we pressed our faces against years ago, at an airport where we'd stand and watch planes taxi on the tarmac, roar down a runway and become vanishing specks in the sky.

Now he circles my wrist with his fingers, his grip a weak cling.

"Hear it?"

His tight mouth, the fixed stare—I think *voices*. Voices in his head. I hear a faint boom. He's pointing at a spot just past the grassy ridge we've walked on, a spot on the hidden hillside.

"An exploding cow," he says, nodding. "Sometimes the head and legs get caught in our fence. Even the guts. Cows die on these slopes, and the farmer can't afford 10,000 schillings for a helicopter to take the body. So he sticks 300 schillings worth of dynamite in the cow's behind and blows it up."

My father offers me a straight face, his eyes unblinking and his mouth shut. I want to laugh, but he looks like he won't. I keep my mirth to myself.

"You don't think it's funny," he says, and spits in the grass.

"I do, but I didn't think *you* thought it was funny."

He takes off ahead of me, arms pumping at his sides, and for a second I stand in the path. His white-and-black figure recedes. I wonder whether I want to follow. But I do. I have to.

We stop at the fence and the path twists onward, around the mountainside. There's a gradual drop on our left.

Coming partly through the fence is a raspberry bush, so I pick and eat some berries. They're sweet. I let them stay in my mouth for a few seconds before I swallow. My father points at shapes on the slope.

Chamois: short, deer-like animals with black legs and tawny bodies. Their hiss is a kind of high-pitched whistle, and they leap over the rocks and away from us, their tails bouncing high. Fascinated, I watch them get away, but sweat stings my right eye. I haven't noticed how hot the day has become. My father gives me a checked handkerchief. We leave the fence, but angle away from the clinic building.

I glance over and see him scratch his head, but otherwise he just ambles along, as if content with the quiet between us. Quite possibly, he has no idea who I am.

Cowbells tinkle from somewhere ahead of us, but I can't see a cow.

I take my father's elbow, forcing him to stop.

"Franz."

Not saying "Dad" or "*Vater*" is easier than I thought.

He spits again.

"My name is Frank. *Franz* takes too long." He gives me a slit-eyed look.

"*Franzzz*," he sneers.

We move off, and I see black goats mottling the slope across the ravine. A wooden house sits in a corner of the field, near the pine forest.

My father stops. He seems to be staring at the goats.

"I fit things," he says, his voice suddenly spirited. He bends down, studies the stones in the path and scoops up four of them. He moves them around in his hand, bends back down and places them on top of a rock. The stones form an upright, freestanding square. No empty spaces.

"I fit things," he repeats. "But I can't fit."

No words come up my throat. Still, I don't think my father wants words. I look at the tall man before me, behind him a huge building spread out and ready to take him back.

He points at the smoke rising from the far house across the ravine.

"That's why the north was best," he says, his voice calm. "You look in all directions and just see trees, bush, sky. Here everyone has to build a flowerbox house and brag about it. And the higher you build, the more you brag."

He starts to walk quickly, swinging his arms. I keep up, matching strides.

"But my house is the highest," he snickers. "Mountain high."

I grab his arm and yank him to a stop.

"I'm Walter."

He holds my gaze, red squiggles in the whites of his eyes. For a second he turns toward the mountains, then puts his face close to mine. Whispers: "And I'm here to be crazy."

"But you—"

He pats my arm, and we step again along the path.

"*Alles in Ordnung*," he declares, his arms swishing at his sides. "Everything in order."

"That's what Mom always said."

"*Said?*"

I realize what my use of the past-tense suggests. "Says," I quickly add. "What she *says*."

He pulls off his glasses and wipes his face with his sleeve.

Before we reach the clinic, we hear another loud noise. It's only a groundskeeper bouncing toward us on his black lawn-mower, but my father and I look at each other and laugh. I guess that he too is imagining a dynamite stick shoved into a dead cow, the lighting of the wick and the farmer's wild dash before the boom and flying flesh.

In the clinic foyer, beneath the ceiling fan, my father shakes my hand. His shut mouth, dry eyes—I don't know what he's thinking.

He gives a slight smile, we both mutter goodbye and he walks away, his shoes clicking on the tiles, his back straight. He pauses once. Something has been announced on the intercom, from a speaker I don't bother to locate. My father's right hand goes to his head, drops back down to his side. He carries on, opens a hallway door and is gone.

I find the film-director nurse at his desk and ask for Franz's diagnosis.

The nurse picks up a pen, lowers his eyes.

"I'm not a doctor. I can't comment on patients."

"But what's your *opinion?*"

He twirls the pen in his fingers, and murmuring voices pass behind me. He raises his head, blinks.

"I'm really sorry. I can't commit myself."

"Is there a doctor I can speak to?"

"Yes, but today she's off."

Herbert meets me in the parking-lot and we drive toward his village, stopping once at a *gasthaus*. It's got timbered ceilings, long wooden benches and tables, a green tiled stove in the middle of the floor and spigoted, wall-set barrels behind the bar. Perhaps this *gasthaus* is like the one where Franz celebrated his homecoming. Hunched-over men sit around us. The only woman is the barmaid, onyx earrings highlighting her blond hair. She could be 25 or 40. She glides between tables, and I wonder how she knows that the men want the beer she brings. Perhaps she's served these men for years, always at the same time, on the same day, at the same bench.

Herbert and I drink our half-litres and he gives evasive answers to my questions about his village life and friendship with my father. He maintains that only he, my mother and I know where Franz is, and that he lives.

"Drink instead of talk," he says, and tips back his glass. He wipes his mouth with his wrist, grabs mine and holds it tight.

"The village you keep asking about—it's full of sick people with bad memories. Thank God, the young ones know nothing. If I could afford it, I'd drive all the old ones up to your father's clinic." Herbert signals the barmaid with two raised fingers.

"I'd go first," he declares, and licks a fleck of beer from his lips.

We arrive at Opa's house and he's standing in his doorway. He's thinner, but has his full head of white hair. He still speaks in rapid dialect, raising his hands and patting the air when he wants to stress a point. I move toward him, the secret of his son like a tire swinging from a branch in my head. I'd promised myself I'd say nothing, but now I hate my promise.

"*Heimkommen!*" he cries. Homecoming! I return his elbow-pumping handshake—his generation doesn't hug—and try not to think too much about what he meant.

The front room is crowded with women in pale flowery dresses and men in dark pants and short-sleeved shirts. All ages are here: small children run around and spill onto the backyard grass. Most of the adults stand or sit with coffee and plates of plum cake. I say hello to face after face, pairs of crinkling eyes and questions. Would I like some cake? Some coffee? Wine? Beer? Am I hungry?

I sit at the kitchen table and find myself alone. People walk in and out, taking bottles of beer or jars of something from the fridge. Herbert gets himself a beer and winks at me, but doesn't sit down. My elbow is close to a half-dozen empty cups and plates of crumbs. They're not the reason I'm here.

I find Opa: he's sitting outside in a metal chair, hands on knees, and he's listening to a dark-haired woman talk. She wears a straw sunhat and sits with her legs crossed, her red leather shoe dangling off her right foot. She's speaking in dialect, so I give up trying to understand her, I just watch the way she touches Opa's wrist while she talks. She notices me and gets up.

"I see him every day!" she says, grinning at me. The woman leaves, heading down the gravel driveway to the lane.

I take her seat, and Opa starts to jabber.

"You're from Vienna?"

"No Opa. Canada. I'm Franz's son, Walter. I'm your grandson."

"Franz is missing!" Opa sticks out his hands and starts to pat the air. "Canada—I was in Canada. I was in his shop every day—but never Franz!"

"I was with you one day. When I was a boy."

"My wife was from Vienna," he states, bringing the palms of his hands together. "She was so slim when I met her. Near the end, she could throw me like a sack into a truck!"

Opa's chest rises and falls, and he dabs the tears of laughter out of his eyes, dabs and dabs. Soon I'm doing the same.

When I return to Montreal, within a day my mother calls. She wants me to visit right away, but won't say why. Typical. I drive my Tercel to Toronto, taking the 401 Highway for as few miles as possible. I drive mostly on Highway 2, then the Thousand Islands Parkway. A grey heron swoops along the St. Lawrence River, its long beak thrust outward, the bird parallel to me for a stretch of road. After the parkway, I navigate a network of winding, doglegging concession roads that make the six-hour trip nine. The roads pass farmhouses, and I glance at their first- and second-floor windows: more crinkling eyes, more questions. More intimacies. I drive by, wondering whether I'll slide into the terminal aloneness some men and women fear. I can't let it happen, though it's already started.

After dealing with the guard at the security hut of my mother's gated community, I park in her underground lot and take the elevator to her apartment. There's no answer when I knock, so I use my key to get in.

"It's Walter!" I shout, and a muffled answer comes from the bathroom.

I make myself an instant coffee in the kitchen and notice the absence of pots and pans on the stove. Yes, the fridge still has a dozen fruit-shaped magnets pinning food-store coupons, emergency phone numbers, pencilled lists of jobs-to-do. Odd: neither the counter nor the table display evidence of meal prep, just a full glass of red wine. The kitchen appears different from the one we shared in my childhood. Back then, I often tried to talk to my mother about my father. I'd stand close, backing her up against the stove and sink and cupboards. I'd try to get her to stop cooking or stowing groceries, rattling pans. Talk was impossible. No matter what my theories were about Daddy being alive, clanking metal against metal was her response—perhaps the noise calmed the clamour in her head.

"There he is," says a voice, and my mother swans toward me with her arms open. Perfume fills the kitchen. I'm in awe—her hair. I can only look down at it, for she's pressed her body against me.

She steps back and I see what she's done: her grey hair is long, thick, wavy, and doesn't move when she does. She's gone to a stylist. As ever, a scarf swathes her neck; the purple sets off her mauve blouse. She wears gold earrings, and her gold ring and watch flash in the kitchen light. Her black skirt goes past her knees. She's put so much effort into looking good, I think there's no way I can mention seeing Franz.

"We'll order a pizza," she proclaims, and gets me a beer from the fridge.

"Mom, you've never ordered pizza in your life."

She twists off the cap, hands me the bottle and a glass. She sits down across from me.

"How would you know what I've ordered?"

"You don't trust how other people cook. Plus you hate wasting money."

She laughs, the cackle that always embarrassed me in public.

"Maybe I wasted too much on Daddy." She sighs.

Her hand quivers when she picks up the wine glass.

"I'm glad you saw him," she adds, and sips. "He was crazy.

I didn't tell you on the phone, because I knew you were coming here."

She just talks on, and my mouth gapes.

"A nurse called Herbert four days ago. With news. A deliveryman had come to the clinic all upset. He said Franz had stepped in front of the speeding truck. The nurse said it happened soon after your visit."

My mother's left hand shakes. Trembles. Her right hand flies overtop of it and holds the hand down.

"You can't be serious!" My shout seems to have no effect. "It's not even true. It can't be true." Inside me, things are falling down.

My mother swallows more wine. "But you know what—the delivery driver said Franz had a smile on his face."

"For 30 years you knew he was alive—and didn't tell me?"

She pushes a lock of hair behind her ear.

"More like six years—Herbert told me. One day Franz just showed up at his house, said he was sick in his head and needed a safe place to live. Herbert arranged the clinic and I used some insurance-money to pay the costs." She stands up, puts her right hand on her hip. "You saw him. I saw him. Now live life."

"But where was he before the clinic?" I move forward and my chest hits the table, shaking the glasses.

"Didn't he tell you? Out west, up north...."

I sneer: "Was he even declared dead—here, in Canada?"

"He was dead to us. Let's not talk about it."

"But Mom—" I can hardly get the words out "—we have to find out what happened. To prove if it was suicide...."

She drops back into the chair, her scarf flying up before it settles again on her neck. I saw a purple scar.

"Walter, the body's been cremated and Herbert's got the ashes. He said that a long time ago, Franz asked him to do it."

Talk is doing nothing. Outside, a lawnmower blares into life. I scratch my head, force myself to stop. My mother just sits, elbows on the table, her chin resting in the palm of her hand.

"Why—" she says quietly, and waits for me to look at her light blue eyes "—don't you have a girlfriend?"

"It's not that easy."

Her voice still fills the air. She asks why I don't visit more, and whether I'll ever come back to Ontario. At one point she gets up and phones for a pizza, replenishes her wine glass. We talk and drink and talk, my mother and I. The pizza arrives, and though we both admit to great hunger, we eat slowly, and sometimes run our greasy fingers under the tap and wipe them off on a dishcloth. Whenever I finish a beer, she gets me another. During our long kitchen night, I make a decision. A secret one. I'll get his ashes. I'll drive them down to where my immigrant father first landed: Halifax. I want to plunge my hands into his ashes and feel their lightness, smear them between my fingers. And I want to see his ashes float, grey specks riding on grey swells. Yes. I'll rent a small boat, motor it offshore and let his ashes loose.

HAROLD HOEFLE teaches at John Abbott College. His work has been published in a number of journals and anthologies, including *The Antigonish Review, Exile, Front& Centre, Grain, Kiss Machine, Matrix, The Windsor Review* and *Telling Stories (New English Stories from Québec)*, as well as in *Cutting*, a four-story chapbook. Hoefle's non-fiction received an Honourable Mention at the 2006 National Magazine Awards. *The Mountain Clinic* is his first book.